A Name that Stuck

The three usual hands shot up into the air from table six when Mrs. Garret asked, "Who said, 'Ask not what your country can do for you, but what you can do for your country.'"

Janie took notice that the hands were raised in correct Prims and Proper order. The Prims and Proper was Janie's little nickname for her tablemates for History. The "Proper" or Amanda's hand was held highest and straightest and with a slight rise of her body lifting out of her seat. While the "Prims" or Kristen and Vanessa's hands were raised a little lower and with slight bends. Vanessa almost needed to slouch so as to not break protocol. As for Janie, the other girl at the table, her hand was raised just enough to prop up her head.

Mrs. Garret studied the classroom as she did every time she asked a question. Sometimes she would pick the most energetic, sometimes she would pick the ones she thought had not done their reading assignment, and every once in a while she would call on Janie.

"So Ms. Kelly," the teacher addressed Janie. "Would you mind letting us know what great American presented us with such a noble request?"

Janie picked up her head as if it were a chore. "Lieutenant John," she paused, "Fitzgerald Kennedy," she finished. She figured most of the kids with the hands up didn't even know his middle name. She would have been more surprised if any knew his rank in the navy.

1

"Very good, Janie," said Mrs. Garret, moving past table six. "You know participation is a part of your grade; you wouldn't want to lose that A just because you were too lazy to raise your hand. Do you know how he got the middle name Fitzgerald?"

"I know it wasn't his father's first name," Janie answered.

The P&P's had stopped kissing up to their teacher and gone back to their usual practice of making faces as other kids talked, especially when it was Janie that was talking. Vanessa was the best at "The Face," though she hated making it and would never do so with Janie in sight. The others tried making it as Janie continued, but it was never a true zombie stare like Vanessa could do.

What Vanessa hated more was "The Name," even if Janie had accepted it.
She hated it because she had created it. It wasn't to be mean. It was before Vanessa joined the ranks of the Prims. The first bus ride to the junior high is where it all started.

That eventful day, Vanessa was the first stop for the bus for all those about to take their first trip to a middle school far far away. She was quite relieved to find herself alone on the bus as she struggled to find a seat where his already tall frame did not seem too gigantic.

Soon two more boys got on and picked seats that made all three in an equal distance from each other as well as keeping the same distance from the driver. If such a design was asked to be made in math class, none of them would have been able to devise the shape. Sometimes the fear of talking to new schoolmates can force the brain to resolve the hardest of calculations.

After one stop at Lithonia Street, the bus driver was clear to head on down to Utopia Parkway and then drive for several miles before stopping at a couple of designated stops for kids that were closer to the school. As the bus stopped at Lithonia, everyone noticed the strange image. Right in front of the large cemetery gates stood a very average looking girl. As Janie passed the bus driver, he shut the doors and took off right away in anticipation of a nice driving stretch. The bus driver's heavy foot on the gas pedal forced Janie to make a quick decision where to sit, and with only one girl on the bus her decision was made without hesitation. She quickly shuffled into the back row right next to Vanessa. She fell in her seat, in part due to the bus driver accelerating through a yellow light.

"Are you alright?" Vanessa asked as she leaned over.

"Yeah, but I hope we make it to school alive," Janie joked.

"My name is Vanessa," the tall girl said, with her and neck and head lurched well above Janie's head even as she slouched.

"Janie," the smaller girl said as she waved her hand.

Vanessa smiled back as she asked, "What school are you from?"

"Thomas Edison PS 109. All my friends are going to I.S. 216. Somehow my mom got me into here. I think it was some kind of lottery for open spots," Janie replied.

"Most of my school went there, too. Only I barely knew anyone. I transferred from a school in Connecticut for part of last year. My dad had to move for work, he was a military officer but now he works for a private defense company. He inspects the parts for them," Vanessa told Janie.

As the girls chatted, the bus flew down Utopia Parkway, then made two more stops on Bell Boulevard before finally reaching the Bay Academy. The Bay Academy was located right where Bell Boulevard begins or ends, depending on your direction. The cul-de-sac in front of the school was filled with cars dropping off their kids.

Bay Academy was a little different than most public schools in the neighborhood as it went from 1st to 8th grade. So there were only a few kids beginning middle school that were not in the Bay Academy for their elementary grades. It also had a high school that most kids attended afterward that was right across the street. Together the two buildings took on a fort type of look. This closed community made it more difficult for new kids.

Janie, Vanessa and the others piled off the bus right in front of the playground where most of the kids were standing around reacquainting with each other. Amanda and Kristen were standing right by the entrance watching all the school buses arrive. They took careful note of those that seemed to be from their grade.

Kristen pointed to Vanessa, the one girl who might be taller than her in class, and pleaded to Amanda to go over and introduce themselves. Amanda agreed, and they went over to say hello. Vanessa was quite overwhelmed by the introduction and completely forgot about Janie. They quizzed her about where she was from, stars she liked, and even how tall she was.

A bell, a very loud alarm type one, rang and a wave of children started for the doors.

Vanessa suddenly remembered Janie. She looked around, noticing she had started for the doors. That's when she said it.

"Janie," she yelled, but Janie didn't respond.

"Hey Cemetery Girl," she said jokingly as Janie turned around. "I will find you at lunch," Vanessa ended.

"Cemetery Girl," Amanda said with a smile and a nod of her head. She looked to Vanessa to show her approval as she added, "Nice one."

And with that the "Prims" were completed, and Janie was tagged "Cemetery Girl."

The Shortcut

All that took place several years ago, five and a half to be exact. The girls had moved across to Bay Academy High School, and although the classes had gotten slightly bigger, the core of students remained the same.

Of the four at the table only Janie had really changed much in that time. She was still friendly with all her class mates, but she had become very much an artist. Janie always assisted in the designing and building of sets for the school's performances, and often her work was picked in contests both in and out of school. She was social, a bit sarcastic, but would spend most her time drawing. It was how she relaxed, and most important, how she expressed herself. She seemed more at ease just letting her art tell you how she was feeling than giving you a verbal update.

This second world was only Janie's, and she liked it that way. She would share some drawings with others, but the closest pictures, the ones that meant the most she would just save in pad after pad. She loved nature and springtime and sometimes would even go into the cemetery across the street to draw. It was like her own park, no one around to bother her.

Vanessa had become one of her best friends, but not the best, that was Bobby. They still took a bus together, but now it was a public one. The Q31 ran straight up Utopia Parkway, and Janie would travel with Vanessa until it passed Dominique's Supermarket. They jumped in a two seater in the rear, and Vanessa stared in wonderment at Janie as she asked, "Captain, Fitzgerald, how in the world did you know that?"

"It was Lieutenant, and hey, I know my presidents, especially the hot ones," she said as she rested her knapsack on her legs, avoiding a semi dried puddle of soda on the floor below the seats.

"How many are there?" Vanessa asked.

"Forty four," Janie answered assuredly.

"There are forty four hot presidents?" Vanessa asked in disbelief.

"Oh, I thought you meant presidents in general," she said. "Only three were hot. Four if you like Abe's beard," Janie said, as they both started laughing and stroking imaginary beards.

"Do you really think Mrs. Garret really knows why his middle name is Fitzgerald?" Janie broke from her laughter with, "Now I'm going to have to go home and Google it. I bet you there was no reason at all."

"Maybe she was the one on the Grassy Knoll," Vanessa said, as she raised her hand pretending to have solved the case.

"Hey, what is a knoll anyways? Have you ever seen a knoll? And who called it a grassy knoll instead of a hill or mound? Now I am going to have to look that up as well." Janie frustrated herself with the question.

"I think it's a hill, with grass," Vanessa said in an attempt to explain a knoll.

"Wouldn't most hills have grass?" Janie asked. She reached over her shoulder and pressed the yellow strip to signal the bus to stop.

"Why are you getting off at Dominique's?" Vanessa asked, surprised to have seen Janie signaling the bus to stop.

"They started opening the back entrance to the cemetery. I cut through it and it saves me a ton of time," Janie explained as she started to rise and throw her knapsack over one shoulder.

"OHHH, you really are Cemetery Girl," Vanessa said in the spooky voice.

"Yeah, have I thanked you enough times for that?" Janie kicked her slightly as she squeezed by Vanessa and out of her seat.

"Let me know if you see a grassy knoll," Vanessa yelled as Janie waved goodbye and stepped off the bus. Crossing Gladwin Street, she made a right and headed straight into the cemetery.

Early spring was Janie's favorite time of the year. And although spring was officially two weeks away, the warm weather had seemed to jump start it a little ahead of the official date. Today was the warmest so far and Janie loved to feel the sun hitting her full force. There was even a little bit of a breeze to enjoy.

Janie slowed her pace down as she entered the gates. She had just remembered that she had never told her mom that volleyball practice was cancelled. Her mother would often run chores on volleyball day, and Janie was sure she would not be home yet. Janie's house keys had disappeared a week ago, and she had not 'fessed up to losing them yet. She realized as she slowed her pace a little more that she was in no hurry.

Janie walked about three fourths of the way through the cemetery when she noticed a large cluster of bright yellow tulips that had already fully grown. She headed down the aisle to get a better view of them. The grave they were placed in front of had a guitar engraved on it that fascinated Janie, and having nothing better to do, she decided to sketch it.

Janie cleared some mud from Saturday's storm off the tombstone. It was still not completely dry and Janie brushed it off her hand on the grass and her knapsack. Turning back to the tombstone she read the name, "Richard Mabbit, Beloved Husband, 1933 to 1963." The guitar was an old style guitar, and the work that went into its carving was really quite detailed.

Janie sat down by the stone and took out her pad. She began to draw the guitar for a while but scratched it out. She flipped the page and started again, this time drawing a young man playing a guitar; it was just too difficult to draw a guitar without someone playing it.

She gave the young man a cowboy hat and a whiskery mustache. The eyes she made large, her trademark in girls she drew, but figured she would try it on the man. Janie's little sidetrack was filling the time she had to wait for her mom, and in no hurry, she spent more time than usual finishing the drawing. When she was finished drawing the man, she studied it. Janie had this feeling it was missing something. Janie would often just draw people without a setting, but for some reason she wanted to add something to the man's drawing. She stared at the drawing for some time and decided to finish it off with a star and a flag on opposite sides of the wall behind the singer. As she started to draw them she was glad how the items added a little country theme to the picture.

Quite involved, she did not notice when a lady approached her. "Young girl," the lady said.

Janie rested her pad and pencil down on the grass, as she started to rise. This was the first time she had ever talked to anyone in the cemetery and was quite disorientated from being pulled from drawing.

"I am so sorry for disturbing you-- I was just curious how you knew my husband?" The lady asked in a very delicate tone.

Janie was now standing next to the elderly lady and, confused by her question, she responded, "Your husband?"

"Richard Mabbit, the Lone Star Tornado, were you a fan? I mean, every once in a while I run into a fan here, but they are usually a little older." The lady looked on the ground at the pad as if she wanted to pick it up.

Janie turned to look at the drawing and then glanced at the tombstone, "Oh no, I am sorry. I was just trying to kill some time." Realizing that 'kill' might not have been the best word, she corrected herself. "I mean I had to wait a half hour before my mom got home, so I just sat down to draw a picture."

The two women couldn't be more opposite. Mrs. Mabbit wore a very conservative long coat, giant orange rimmed glasses and grayish white hair cropped around her face.

Janie was in a hooded navy blue sweatshirt unzipped, with a shirt with a graffiti like decal that said "Save the Planet," wearing two different colored Converses, one black and one dark blue with red stripes. Unlike the lady, Janie's hair was thick, so thick it would often drive her crazy. Janie hated it, yet everybody always would say how lucky she was. Both images seemed somewhat at home in the cemetery but were in contrast to each other like a sailor and a baby boy playing in the sand would look at the beach. The Goth wannabe and the widow continued their conversation.

"But the likeness." The woman went over and picked up the pad. She continued with a touch of sincerity that expressed years of true love, "It's almost like I'm looking at his picture when we first met. He had such big loving eyes. He was such a lovely person."

She ran her fingers over the drawing as if she was touching someone's face. "And that silly mustache," she laughed. "It took me years to get him to shave it off. I miss it so much."

Janie felt kind of awkward, but what she felt most of all was sad for the elderly lady. The lady was probably about seventy five. She was very thin and tall. Janie loved the mix of her gray and white hair and almost commented on it, but instead stayed on the topic of Mrs. Mabbit's husband.

"He must have been very rich and famous," Janie said encouragingly.

"Oh, how I wish," the lady said. "No, he was a studio performer. He recorded with quite a few big-time acts. All the big stars of the day, but the studio people, they do not really become famous, or rich. They have some fans, the real music fans. They come by here once in a while, and leave things like flowers or notes. At least I think they do, maybe I just imagine they are fans and that they leave things."

"Well, you can have the picture. I had just finished it up." Janie took her pad back from Mrs. Mabbit and gently began tearing out the page.

The lady's face grew very excited. "Let me give you something for it." She reached into her bag and pulled out a wallet. The wallet was crammed with coupons and the lady fiddled through them till she finally found a dollar. She grabbed Janie's arm and forced the dollar into her palm.

"Really, it's free," Janie said as she shook her hand in a display that she did not want to accept the bill.

"Take it, please. I just wish I could give you more."

Janie finally accepted the dollar. Laughing to herself, she thought about the irony of her first paying job as an artist. There are a whole lot of old ladies in the cemetery; maybe she found her niche, she jokingly thought.

Janie glanced at her cell phone and realized it was just about four o'clock. Her mom still wouldn't be home, but Bobby would be home from school and she could hang at his house.

"I am sorry about your husband," Janie said as she started to head back to the paved road.

"Thank you. My name is Arlene and thank you so much for the picture." The lady raised her voice a little to make sure Janie heard.

"Really, you didn't need to pay me." Janie stopped walking and turned around as she stated it one more time.

"Hush. I wish I could have given you more. Go buy yourself a soda or something," was the last thing Mrs. Mabbit said as they both waved bye to one another.

Soda, Janie said to herself as she started to walk away again. Not without a senior discount. Anyway, it really did brighten up her day to know she made somebody so happy. She couldn't wait to tell Bobby and picked up the pace to get to his house.

Quite a Coincidence

Bobby always got home at four. He was in five different extra activities, one for each day of the week. Monday it was math team; Tuesday robotics club; Wednesday was student government; Thursday he tutored for extra credit. She had asked him once what he did with the extra credit as he had straight A's, but he just said something about Princeton liking to see you did things like that. Janie wasn't sure what he did on Friday, but she was sure it wasn't the baseball or football team.

Bobby wasn't very athletic. He had a little X Game ability, and he could handle a skateboard. He was even a ham on his bike, but put a ball in his hands and most likely it would slip right out and fall on the ground.

Janie sprang up the three steps of the Wu's front porch. She did a quick two rings of the doorbell. Opening the screen door she brought her lips right up to the peephole.

When she heard Bobby flip the latch, she blew raspberries through her mouth at the peephole to scare Bobby.

Bobby opened the door before Janie had stopped blowing the raspberries.

"You realize you're fogging up the peepholes, not to mention that I can smell your breath through the door."

"Guess what happened to me today?" Janie excitedly asked as she busted into the living room.

Bobby, trying to imitate Janie's excitement, answered, "You got hit in the head with volleyball."

"No, no practice today. I was on my way home through the cemetery. I stopped by a tombstone and drew a picture. It was the guy buried there. Well, that's what his wife told me."

"Who's wife?" Bobby asked.

"The dead guys wife, she was visiting his grave," Janie replied quickly.

"What grave?" Bobby riffled off as quickly as Janie had replied.

"The grave I stopped at to draw the picture," Janie retorted without a breath.

Bobby took a breath for effect and maybe just to catch up in his head. "She's probably a nut," he stated abruptly.

"Of course she's nuts, but she gave me a dollar for the picture," Janie said as she took out the dollar and stretched it in and out a couple of times for effect.

"Hey, maybe we can open a business. There are a lot of crazy widowed old ladies out there"

"I already did the math. That would be one million drawings to make a million. I ain't got enough pencils," Janie said with a little smirk.

Putting up his right hand and cupping his chin and refusing to give up on the idea he said, "Yeah, we'll have to go for the rich and famous ones."

They had worked their way into the den. Janie threw herself on the couch, as Bobby sat down in the computer chair and spun it around to face Janie. Even from inside the den you could tell it was an addition to the house and not part of the original construction. Janie and Bobby loved the room and it is where they would almost always hang out.

"He was famous. Apparently he was a musician. Well, not really famous, but he played with famous people," Janie said excitedly.

Bobby kicked off with his leg and spun the chair again, this time letting his arm slam against the desk as it stopped him with his body facing the computer. "So lay the name on me."

"Richard," Janie said pausing for a second. "I think his last name was Mabbit, or something like that. Yeah that was it. Richard Mabbit, he was a guitar player. The Lone Star."

"The Lone Star Tornado," Bobby interrupted. "Am I good or what?"

The printer started buzzing as Bobby hit some more keys and said, "Let's see if we can find an obituary. Here we go. Richard Mabbit, an accomplished guitarist known as the Lone Star Tornado, died November 22, 1963." Bobby's voiced raised with astonishment as he continued, "Wow, November 22, 1963. Do you know what day that was?"

"Saturday," Janie played along not realizing the significance of the date.

"No, it was a Friday; it's also the day JFK was assassinated."

Janie's eyes opened wide. "That's funny."

"What's funny?" Bobby said, as he spun the chair again to face the now quieted printer.

"Vanessa and I were talking about JFK and the grassy knoll on the way home." Janie shrugged her shoulder. "It's just funny weird."

Bobby snatched the paper from the printer, glanced at it quick and slammed it in Janie's open hand as he said, "Ladies and Gentleman, The Lone Star Tornado."

Janie's face turned white. "This is not funny," she said.

"What's all this funny not funny stuff, feels like some kind of inverted déjà vu."

Janie, not paying any attention to what Bobby was jabbering about, just stared at the picture. "That's the man I drew!"

Bobby paused and then dismissed Janie's comment. "Well of course that is who you drew. It is the Lone Star Twister after all." Bobby made sure to mangle his nickname.

"No Bobby, that's the man I drew, right down to that crazy looking mustache," Janie still not having moved since she first saw the picture.

Bobby snatched the paper back from Janie. "What are you losing it to? Wow, look at those eyes, it looks like they're bigger than his head. They should have called him Lone Star Owl! You drew this freak?"

Bobby spun around again and launched more files to the printer.

"Hey, this guy really recorded with some big people. Frank Sinatra, Louie Armstrong, even Jerry Lee Lewis."

"Enough with the Texas Foghorn. It's creeping me out. Hey, Do you know JFK's middle name?" Janie asked, needing a break from the excitement of the day.

"Fitzgerald, was her mom's last name. I am smarter than a fifth grader, Janie," Bobby added, annoyed by Janie's doubt that he would not know. Janie pumped her fist, happy she had found her answer. Yet she was still somewhat disappointed that she apparently could not keep up with Bobby's retention of facts read on the internet.

"Oh you're so know-it-all aren't you? Well then, who called it the grassy knoll?" Janie's eye twinkled as she asked the question. "And what is a knoll for that matter?"

Bobby froze in shock. He spoke very slowly with his voice breaking, "I don't know, and I don't know, well I know it's a hill of some sort, but exactly I don't know." Bobby turned to the computer and gazed at it to let it know he had some work for them to do. He swung back around to face Janie. "It's getting late, and I am going to be real busy tonight, now."

"I will talk to you on Saturday." Janie left Bobby to his hours of research.

Another Meeting

One week had passed since Janie drew the Tornado. Bobby had emailed her over twenty sites referencing the Kennedy assassination, many with Grassy Knoll facts. He also sent a bunch of other sites mentioning Richard Mabbit's guitar playing on different songs and albums. Janie had read them all and was becoming quite involved in building theories about the assassination. Janie did not mention her meeting with Mrs. Mabbit to anyone else but was finding all the information quite exciting. It quite easily filled her spare time for the rest of the week.

The very next Monday found Vanessa and Janie once again riding the Q31 instead of spiking volleyballs in the gym. "So do you think we will ever have practice again? " Vanessa said in a frustrated tone.

"What happened? I actually thought we were supposed to today."

"Coach Hill has the flu. She and two students went home this morning," Vanessa informed her. "Hey, find your keys yet?"

"No, and I know my mom is going to be out." Janie was annoyed that she was again locked out of her house for the foreseeable future, or at least till 4:30.

"Come over to my house."

"No, I got a ton of reading to do for the book report. I'll just sit in the backyard and get it done." Janie told Vanessa in a defeated tone. Janie loved to read the internet or magazines, even text books. Anything where absorbing facts was involved, she loved to read, but reading a novel was a chore and a half.

The bus pulled up to the stop in front of Dominique's Supermarket. Janie hugged Vanessa goodbye, and jumped off the bus. Just like last week, she turned down Gladwin Street and entered the backside of Cavalier Cemetery. Richard Mabbit's tombstone was almost on the other side of the cemetery, and as she headed that way she started thinking about her meeting last week. It was the only person she had ever spoken to in the cemetery, and aside from one popular area near the middle of the cemetery, she did not recall ever seeing anyone else in her journeys. The popular area that Janie had often noticed was about halfway through the cemetery, and once again there were a couple of people there. They always seemed to be in the same facility, but too far too really make the people out.

Janie was getting closer to Mr. Mabbit's tombstone. When she turned the corner, she saw it and Mrs. Mabbit as well. Janie stopped walking; she really had not expected to see her and was not really sure if she wanted to. She ducked behind the bush, and thought about it for a minute.

She decided to stay on the road to the right, and hopefully Mrs. Mabbit would not see her. The road swerved a little out of the way, but she was really not prepared to face Mrs. Mabbit. She turned right and walked at a quick pace, but about thirty seconds in she heard Arlene's voice.

"Janie, Janie," she yelled, "Come here. I must talk to you."

Janie thought for a second about just ignoring her, but she realized that wasn't going to work. In no time Arlene Mabbit was upon her. She moved pretty fast for her age, but she was also almost running and out of breath by the time she reached Janie.

"Janie, I am so glad I saw you. That picture, it was amazing." Mrs. Mabbit was simply glowing. It made Janie very happy to see her so filled with such joy.

"I know. Actually my friend Bobby.. We looked him up online. The picture I drew looked just like him," Janie said, assuming that Arlene was referring to the likeness of the etching.

"And you thought I was crazy." Arlene jokingly continued, "Admit it."

"Yeah, but now I think we're just both crazy. Bobby still doesn't believe me."

"Well, you can tell Bobby this," she went on. "That star you drew in the background. I didn't notice it at first, but when I got home there was this plaque. Right in our hallway, was this plaque, and they were identical." Arlene took a deep breath and then continued, still filled with excitement. "It was right there all the time, only I didn't know what I was looking for. Actually, I knew what I was looking for; I just had no idea where to look."

"I don't understand," Janie stated. She was pleased to hear that the star reminded her of something at her house, but she really couldn't comprehend why it would make Mrs. Mabbit so happy.

"Richie had recorded some tunes in our basement with a young performer from Texas in the fifties. He had a little studio down there, and the young boy was just starting out. He was just the nicest boy; well, he stayed over the whole weekend. We were just married; I think he might have been our first guest who ever stayed over. That young's boy's name was Buddy Holly."

Janie knew the name. "He was a rock star."

"Yes, he was," Arlene went on. "Taken much too soon. My husband never felt right about releasing the tapes. It was too soon he said. Richie felt it wasn't respectful, and he was sure that other versions of the songs would appear. Besides, he would always say we needed something to retire on. And then like that, 13 years later he was gone as well."

"Same day as JFK." Janie chimed in, showing her research.

"You really did do you homework, didn't you?" She looked at Janie in a proud way. "I tore that house apart for forty years. I dug holes in the backyard before I finally gave up and figured they were lost forever. Like I said, I didn't know where to look until you drew that picture.

"For forty years those tapes sat in the little compartment of that star. I never knew it even had a compartment. I am meeting with somebody next week. They are going to give me a lot of money for the recordings. Three original unreleased songs written and recorded by Buddy Holly Janie, that is what your drawing lead me too."

Janie looked at Arlene in complete shock. "I am so happy for you," she said.

"I told you I wish I could give you more, please take this." Arlene started tucking two tens into Janie's jacket pocket. So overwhelmed by the events, Janie didn't even protest as Arlene finished stuffing the bills deep into her pocket. They talked for a while about her husband. Arlene cried when she told Janie abut that horrible Friday in November.

Soon, Janie mentioned that she had an extra amount of homework and that she needed to go. They hugged and promised to keep in touch. Janie speed walked away. She in part wanted to stay longer, but had she stayed much longer she would not have been able to head to Bobby's house. Janie made it to his house in half the time that it would if she was walking at a normal pace. She was so excited that she didn't even bother to make a face when he answered the door.

"Volleyball cancelled again?" asked Bobby as he swung open the door.

Janie barely let him get his words out as she pushed him straight through the living room and kitchen, slamming him through the half open door into the den.

"I saw her again, Mrs. Mabbit."

"What, did she have you draw her long lost puppy?" Bobby continued without sincerity, "Janie, we already went through this. It was a coincidence."

"I drew something in the background. The thing I drew. It was in the woman's house. It led her to find her husband's lost tapes."

"She is probably making it up in her head," Bobby said.

"Yes, and maybe she made up the twenty bucks she gave me." Janie pulled out the money and slammed it into Bobby's palm. "What do you got to say now?"

"Holy Franklin, maybe there really is a market for this drawing dead people thing," Bobby said, "and bigger than you think, Janie. This is two hundreds."

Janie looked at the two bills frozen in Bobby's hand. It was the most money she had ever seen in her life, and she had no idea what to do with it.

"Bobby, you have to hide it for me. How would I ever explain it? How would I explain any of this? My dad would probably go out and have Mrs. Mabbit arrested." Janie collapsed on the couch as Bobby lowered himself into the computer seat, still holding the $200 like a bomb that might explode. He turned and looked at Janie, instructing her to tell him exactly what Mrs. Mabbit said. Janie, both excited and nervous, detailed her whole conversation with Arlene.

"This is all too weird. We have to test it." Bobby sounded very serious about his proposal to help in analyzing Janie's ability.

"How in the world can we test it?" Janie asked.

"I don't know, I will think of something, but Saturday – one way or another, we are going to test it. There must be some logical explanation."

The Test

It was hard, but Janie managed to keep her mind on the history quarterly during the school week, and, if not checking the top 100, Janie spent most of her time studying for it. Soon enough, Friday and the history test finally was upon them. Janie looked over at Vanessa to see if she looked nervous. Vanessa was nonchalantly looking through a People magazine. Janie quipped to herself that at least it had a small picture of Obama's daughter on the cover.

History was the second to last class on Friday, and when that test ended all Janie could think about was the really important test tomorrow. Janie was a little troubled that for the first time in her life she wasn't going to study. She looked over at Vanessa, who smiled, handed Mrs. Garret her paper and then went back to her magazine.

The last class seemed to take an eternity but finally the bell rang and Janie and Vanessa headed to the bus station, having survived another history exam. Now Janie could concentrate on the exam that only she was taking.

Saturday morning arrived in a flash and Janie not fully ready to embrace it started to stir slowly in her bed. As she tossed, Janie started getting excited about the test. She had no idea what Bobby had planned, but the possibility of the supernatural had gotten her very excited.

Janie dressed a little for the role today, more black than usual, though black was easily thirty percent of her wardrobe. Janie wasn't allowed to wear makeup, but she had acquired a stash over the last year. She grabbed her mirror and eyeliner and threw them in her bag.

Janie had guitar at 11:30am. It was usually a chore for her parents to get her out of bed in time to make it. Sometimes she went with the sweatpants she had woken up in 10 minutes prior, and most of that time was used in a battle with her hair. Her dad was quite surprised to see her pop dwn the stairs at 11:15, guitar in hand.

Bobby would also not be described as Saturday go getter. Even with all the excitement of the test Bobby couldn't make it down till 11:20 in the morning. He stopped at the bottom of the stairs to scratch his dog Wendy on the belly for a couple of minutes. When the dog had enough it broke free and went upstairs. Bobby grabbed his folder full of names and information and looked through it as he shoved down some Honeycombs on the living room couch.

Saturday might have come quickly for Janie, but today's guitar lesson was agonizing and endless. With all the excitement of the last week she had not practice at all, and her fingers were throbbing as she tried to squeeze out a chord. Her fingers' pain was emphasized by the dark nail color she had put on last night.

The B minor chord rang out like a wounded cat in an alley, and her guitar teacher, Stan, upon hearing it, decided it was close enough to 12:30 to end the lesson. Janie raced to the car and headed back home.

They met at Bobby's house and headed to the cemetery. Bobby brought the folder full of research, and Janie had a sketch pad and couple of pencils. Bobby led her deep inside, and referring to a crude mappish drawing guided her to the tombstone of Regina Wilson. The tombstone was very pretty with a floral design around the border, but unlike Mr. Mabbit's tombstone, unless the lady was a florist there was no hint about the lady's life. Bobby instructed her to sit down and draw whatever she felt. Bobby sat down next to Janie and concentrated intently. After a few minutes he pulled out a Sudoku puzzle from his folder and started to do it. After another ten minutes Bobby finished the puzzle, and Janie said she was done with the drawing. She ripped it out of her sketch pad and handed it to him. It didn't take long to look over the picture, that of a great big poodle. He placed the drawing inside his folder and pulled back out his map.

Referring to his map and leading the way, they once again started to wander around the cemetery.

"So are we done?" Janie asked. "Did I pass?"

"No we are not, one down two to go," Bobby said, a little irritated.

He led her near the middle of the cemetery, and Janie pointed out to him, the area where she always saw people. Once again there was an old lady accompanied by a tall man in the general location.

After a few more aisles they found the next testing area. Janie sat down by the grave.
The rather plain tombstone was that of a husband and wife who had both passed several years ago. Once again Bobby

sat silent for a few minutes, making sure Janie was settled, and then pulled out another Sudoku puzzle. Janie studied the tombstone; its side was rough, intentionally left like that for effect. The marker itself was very plain, no designs, and simply the husband's and wife's names. Even though Janie took a little time before drawing, this time Janie finished first. "Who's taking a test here? Come on already," Janie said anxiously as Bobby finally put down his puzzle.

Just like the previous time, Bobby studied the picture. It was a street scene with a few cars and a garbage truck blocking the middle of the road. Bobby simply put the drawing in his folder and took out his map. He helped Janie up and started to head to the third testing area.

The last site was just a couple of aisles over. Following the same routine as before, they sat down, Janie started to draw and soon Bobby started another Sudoku puzzle. Bobby beat Janie this time and peeked over her shoulder as she was finishing.

This time Janie drew a young girl, in the similar fashion to many drawings she had done before. Bobby looked at the portrait quickly then put it in the folder with the other drawings as he said, "Let's head for my house; we can discuss the results there."

By the time they got to Bobby's house, it was already 3:30. After talking to Bobby's mom for a few minutes, updating her on the Bay Academy and volleyball, they headed to the back room. Janie jumped on the couch as Bobby took his usual spot on the computer chair. He laid out the drawings on the desk.

"So how did I do?" Janie asked as she got up and stood over his shoulder.

"You have to understand, to my knowledge there are no standard tests for this type of thing," Bobby said in a serious voice. "So here is what I decided to do. I researched quite a few people at the cemetery, finding a great detail about their lives."

"Then you just see if I drew something important from their lives." Janie started to follow the logic.

"That is what I originally had planned. Then I remembered you told me that originally you were just drawing the guitar. Something told you to do more. Something told you what to draw. It was the wife. She was asking him like she asked him so many times before. Where are the tapes?"

"You mean I wasn't the one contacting Richie?" Janie tried to grasp what Bobby was alluding to.

"Exactly! You are just the device they are communicating with. The first woman we visited, she raised dogs. She even had a dog that placed in the Westminster Dog Show. It was the pride of her life. It was also a great big Standard Poodle."

"Like the one I drew," Janie proudly chimed in.

"I'm not a dog expert, but it looks just like him. Right as you were getting ready to draw I asked her to show me the joy of her life."

"What about the street scene?" Janie was very excited now and almost pushing Bobby out of his seat to get a better look at the pictures she drew.

"That man worked forty years as a garbage man. Before you started drawing, I asked him to tell me what he did. Why did you draw the street?"

"I don't know. I just suddenly was compelled to draw some street that I was on a couple of days ago. At least I think it was, there was some kind of truck on it. I didn't remember exactly what, so I made it a garbage truck."

"What about the little girl?" Janie asked wondering about test number three.

"That's the wildest part," Bobby said as he held the third picture up a little so Janie could see without knocking him off the chair.

"Well, for the last one I didn't ask the person to show me anything. He was a musician just like Mr. Mabbit. No family, not married, I could find no reason to think that he would inspire you to draw a little girl. I think you just drew something, I don't think there was a connectrion because there was no contact." Bobby handed Janie the last drawing as he continued speaking. "Yes Janie, you passed the test. Only let's be serious. Who could we possibly share this with?"

"No one would believe us. It is just so frustrating," Janie agreed with Bobby. "Anyway at least we know."

"We can't really ever be sure. I think for now we should try to forget about it."

"I don't think that it's that easy to forget," Janie retorted.

"I mean we should try to let it rest for now. I will try to think of something, some way that you can prove it to the world. If that is what you want to do."

"I don't know, I am so confused. My dad already thinks I am Goth. Bobby, I am not Goth, am I?" Janie looked at Bobby sad and confused.

Bobby paused for a moment, he looked down at his Sudoku puzzle and mused to himself how much life is more complicated than random numbers. He would usually just blurt out any answer anytime and be confident it was right. Debates or anything, it didn't matter. He could formulate a brilliant coherent answer in a second. But this wasn't a debate. No, it was more important than that; he looked at the puzzle for some time. Then gathered his strength and looked right into Janie's eyes and said, "You are a ray of sunshine. If anything you are the opposite of Goth. They carry death out into the live world; you fill things with life again. Besides, you accessorize your black with other colors."

A Rift at School

The morning bus rides were always a highlight of the day for Janie. She got to hang with Vanessa by herself without the other Prim or Proper. Vanessa and Janie were talking about the hottest topic of late in the Bay Academy. The arrival of Keith was the only thing any female junior was talking about. He was new to the school and to the state, arriving to both about a month ago. It was claimed by some, including Vanessa, that he was the hottest boy to ever have graced Bay Academy. Keith Jackal was a laid back surfer type straight from California. He still had the tan, and shark tooth and twine necklace. He also had one thing that only three other kids in their grade had a car.

"Did you see him pull away yesterday?" Vanessa asked.

"He looked a lot like the day before, Vanessa, you are obsessing," Janie said as she nudged Vanessa a little for her to pull the bus signal.

"I wonder if he drove it from California." Vanessa started to daydream but snapped back to reality with a direct question; "But you think he's cute?" Vanessa paid careful attention to Janie's response, concerned about Janie's rating of the new boy in town and hoping she showed no interest.

"Yes, Vanessa, he's cute. Cute and a toot"

"What does that mean?" Vanessa inquired, quite concerned that Keith might be ATOOT. She did not like the sound of that at all and also wondered how Janie would know.

"Oh, I don't know, can we change the topic?" Janie begged Vanessa as the bus waited at the light right in front of the Bay Academy's school yard.

"Tomorrow is the bike fund raising trip. Are you going?" Vanessa gave into Janie's pleas and changed topics.

"Yeah, I can't wait; it is such a great idea. An actual school trip on bikes. It is the first time they are doing it." Janie added to the excitement.

"So do you think Keith will be there? I hope he had a bike when he moved."

"He must have had a bike. He lived in California. That's all they do. You can't walk anywhere. He could not have been driving for to long."

"Did you ever wonder why Keith has a car? Do you think he was left back?" Vanessa once again started obsessing about the new heart-throb in town.

The bus pulled up in front of the Bay HS and the girls jumped out. Janie glanced at her cell phone and said, "We only have two minutes." They took off in a mad sprint for the front doors. Janie Kelly and Vanessa Craven have had the same homeroom classes since they first met, and it never seemed as exciting as now. Homeroom 1124 suddenly became the most walked by, window shopped class with the sudden appearance of Keith Jackal.

The girls raced to the door, Janie slamming through it in a comedic way that caused her classmates to giggle. Vanessa stopped a few feet before entering, and fixed her hair and shirt before strutting into the class just as the bell rang.

Vanessa walked to her desk, which was aligned to the right of Keith's. Last week all the desks had to reshuffle as Ms. Freeman insisted on alphabetical order. Janie now sat in the first row and was not happy about her new location.

"I hope all those who are going on the bike tour of the old motor highway have brought their permission forms." Almost all the kids handed in the forms, including Keith.

Keith raised his hand, "Are we allowed to meet at the site or do we have to meet at the school?"

"You should notify us if you are planning to meet us at the start," Ms. Freeman said in such a manner that displayed her annoyance with continually updating the class with the bikathon's rules and regulations. She finished the update with the meeting time, reminder to bring a helmet and other safety issues.

Keith leaned over to Vanessa and asked if she and CG were going to the park or school first. She told him that they were both closer to the site than the school.

"I was thinking," Keith started to say.

"Mr. JAC-KAL!" Ms. Freeman chimed in. Ms. Freeman was also the head of the art division. She was not very tall, and when frustrated like now would often throw back her short black hair with her hand. "We do not make small talk when the teacher is talking. Such actions in the future will put you in detention."

Vanessa looked heart broken as she could only, until the end of homeroom, dream of what he was about to ask. Time can seem much longer than it really is; the next ten minutes took an eternity for Vanessa as she tried not to keep peeking over at Keith.

The bell for first class sounded and Vanessa leapt out of her desk like an animal escaping a trap. She almost knocked Keith right out of his desk.

Keith grabbed her arm, in part to get her attention and in part to keep from falling.
And then Vanessa's heart dropped a little as Keith, holding her arm, said, "CG! Come over here."

Keith had picked up on the Cemetery Girl and had shortened it to CG. Janie actually found it kind of cute, and after all it was less annoying than the full name.

Janie turned around and headed to the back of the class.

"Well, I was thinking, if you two aren't heading to the school, I could drive over by where you guys live and we could bike from there."

"I was actually planning to ride over with my father. He might be a chaperone," Janie was saying as she was suddenly kicked by Vanessa. "Oh, but what I meant to say was he can't. He has to work. So what do you think V?"

"YES! I mean Yes Well, of course I MEAN YES. You know it sounds like fun."

"Great, we'll call it a date." Keith winked at the girls, grabbed his books and headed to Science.

Janie started to head to the door, but Vanessa just stood there. Janie returned to Vanessa's immobile body.

"Do I have a date with Keith?" Vanessa asked in a dreamlike state that she was scared she was going to wake up from.

"Yes, Yes I mean, yes we do" Janie replied sarcastically. "We also have History class, Come on, you know how Mrs. Garret is."

Table six was alive with talk when Vanessa announced to the P&P's that she was going to travel with Keith to the start of the bike trip. Amanda was quite excited to have the new kid as part of her touring group. She was dating Tom, the star pitcher and leading scorer on the basketball team. Kristen did not take it as well. "I am not surprised the way you have been hanging all over him," she said.

Janie was about to interject that she was also going on a date with Keith, but she didn't want to fan any more flames for Kristen.

Ms. Garret came over to table six and asked if they were done yet, and the girls quieted down.

The day flew by and every time Vanessa and Janie were together, all Vanessa talked about was Keith. Janie was beginning to get pretty annoyed, even if he was cute.

Last period was art, and Keith, Vanessa and Janie were all in it together. Keith came over to the girls and asked, "So where do you guys live?"

"We're both over by the cemetery on Booth Memorial," Janie said, fearing that Vanessa's answer would take ten minutes.

"I am actually by the hospital on Booth," Vanessa interjected, wanting to be part of the conversation.

"Who's closer to the trail?"

"I am," Janie answered, as she shot a bit of a stare at Vanessa.

"Well then I will park by you and we can all ride to the trail." Keith looked at Janie, and Janie got the feeling that Keith was glad that they would meet by her house.

The bell blared, and everyone piled into the last class of the day.

Ms. Freeman was at the door as the three walked by. "Oh, look, my little sheep have returned to their shepherd as the day ends," she joked as they passed by. "Remember Mr. Jackal, detention is a lonely place on a Friday," reminding him of his earlier mistake of talking while she was addressing the class.

"Today we are going to partner you up, and each of you is going to draw your partner." As she spoke Ms. Freeman went around the room pointing to two people at the same time, and then directing them to easels that faced each other. "So take out you graphite, and we be using the large paper today."

There were only four people left unpaired: Kristen, Vanessa, Janie and Keith. Vanessa started to twitch a little nervously until Ms. Freeman pointed to her and Kristen at the same time. Both faces pouted and then stared at each other with blank stares, to put it nicely.

Janie thought to herself how scary those two drawings were going to turn out. She wondered if Kristen would draw horns on the top of Vanessa's head. She then turned to Keith and once again got the feeling that Keith was happy to have gotten the partner that he did. She felt her cheek in an attempt to see if she was blushing when he was not looking, and even thought about taking out her mirror to check on her appearance.

"So who's going to go first?" Keith asked aloud to Ms. Freeman in a macho way.

Ms. Freeman jumped in and said, "No time for that, class, you are going to have to situate your easels so that each can view the other."

Janie took a good look at Keith. His eyes were bluer than the sea he surfed. And his face was filled with such

36

sincerity. Most of the lines that Janie drew were downward. She often started to draw someone from the top of their heads and worked down.

Keith had finished first and was now just posing for Janie. The other two at the table were scratching so hard on the paper that you could see the graphite falling on the floor. The class was just about to end when Janie finally finished. She took the pad from off the easel and turned it to show Keith.

"WOW," Keith said. "And allow me to add I do not use that word lightly like most other surfers. When I say WOW I mean WOW! And I mean WOW," he said as he brushed his hand close to the painting.

Keith studied the drawing for a couple seconds more before grabbing his pad.

"What do you think?" he asked. "I think they go together pretty well," as he turned around his drawing.

"WOW!" Janie said in amazement. The drawing was fantastic; it was quite similar to Janie's in size. Janie studied it and really thought he had captured her quite well, down to the smirk she was so proud of.

They turned around to see Kristen and Vanessa, who were showing each other their creations.

"Ugh," Vanessa grunted as Kristen turned her pad around. Janie almost busted out into laughter.

"Vanessa doesn't have a Uni-brow," Keith said in a very joking tone.

The Old Motor Road

Vanessa arrived at 10:30am, a good half hour before Keith was supposed to park around the corner from Janie's house. She wanted to make sure she was there before Keith arrived. Janie, on the other hand, was just pulling the blankets off from over her head.

Janie jumped into the clothes laid out on her bed without much thought. She threw on a bright orange shirt and a black pair of stretch pants that her mom had laid picked out the night before. Her mother had put out the orange shirt to aid in cars spotting her. Janie would usually pick her own clothes but was rushing so quickly she threw them on. Janie wasn't sure if she was more excited about the ride or seeing Keith, but now that she was up she was completely pumped about the day ahead.

She was not surprised to see Vanessa waiting in the dining room talking to her mom, as she bounded down the stairs. She grabbed a banana from a bowl on the dinning room table and started to peel it.

"Are you ready?" Vanessa impatiently asked.

"All set," Janie said and took a bite from the banana.

"Got your cell phone, Janie?" her mother asked.
"Remember to call me when you get to the starting site."

"I know mom," Janie annoyingly replied.

"What time will it be over?" her mom asked, looking for a piece of paper to write down the time and anything else of importance.

"Around three, I think. We should be home by four at the latest." Janie had added some time for her to spend with Keith and Vanessa.

"Well, call me on my on my cell when you are heading home. You have your key with you?" Janie's mom asked, reminding Janie of her key trouble.

"Yeeess!!" She lied looking at Vanessa to make sure she did not mention losing it.

She kissed her mom goodbye and then she and Vanessa exited the house through the side door heading to the garage. Vanessa had parked her mountain bike in the backyard by the garage and hopped on it while Janie went to get hers. They both shot out of the driveway and down Pigeon Meadow Road.

They followed Pigeon Meadow Road which ran along the cemetery and at the corner turned down Lithonia till they came to the cemetery gates. There Keith was waiting, bike lying on the ground next to his car. Keith was decked in California surf gear, a t-shirt with an un-buttoned shirt over it. His jeans, with a couple of worn holes, looked that they had been perfectly faded by a type of sun that New York has never known.

Vanessa got Keith's attention and decided to show off a little bit by pedaling with no hands. As she got close to the car Vanessa's bike swayed a little bit, and she slammed into Keith's car. Keith was watching them intently and ran over to make sure that Vanessa was alright. For the most part, she seemed more embarrassed than anything else.

Janie looked and saw that the crash had left a little dent on the car, but Keith never really looked at it, showing more concern about Vanessa. He helped her untangle herself from the bike and then helped her up. He picked up the bike, bouncing it back down on its tires making sure that it was rideable.

"I think that's why the bike has handle bars," Keith said smiling. "Lucky you didn't crack your head open." Vanessa looked sheepishly at Keith and apologized about hitting his car.

After Vanessa had shaken off the cobwebs they all mounted their bikes and headed off for the trail.

"Should we shoot through the cemetery?" Janie asked.

"OOHH," Keith said as he turned around and made a zombie stare that was almost as good as Vanessa's. "You really are Cemetery Girl aren't you?"

Janie laughed and Vanessa somehow felt that all those years of doing the stare behind her back had been slightly lifted. Janie had seen the stare and laughed. Vanessa was always scared that Janie would see her doing the stare first, but now that worry was over.

Taking off into the cemetery, Keith was in the lead by a good distance.
Vanessa rode up next to Janie. "That stare was pretty funny," she said, wanting to make sure Janie acknowledged it.

"Yeah, he almost does it as good as you. Vanessa, I saw you do it a couple of times. I know you don't mean it. Really, it's okay."

"You're a great friend. Better than me," Vanessa admitted in a soft voice.

"Hey, what was all that no hand stuff about?" Janie asked, trying to get off the topic.

"I was trying to make an impression." Vanessa kind of chuckled her lame response as they both pedaled deeper into the cemetery.

"An impression?" You left a dent on his car. That's kind of an actual impression. Does that count?" Janie smirked.

"Thanks!" Vanessa laughed as she pedaled faster and caught up with Keith.

Janie was about to speed up as well when she suddenly noticed something or someone over by the area she so often noticed people congregating. She quickly looked away and, being in the cemetery for the first time since seeing Mrs. Mabbit, her mind thought about all the craziness of the last couple of weeks. She had kind of stopped thinking about all that since Keith had showed up at school and caused so much gossip.

Her reminiscing was quickly interrupted when Keith yelled, "Hurry up CG or they will leave without us." As she rode through back half of the cemetery all her thoughts again started to swirl around Keith. Just like the night before, it was like her mind could not contain itself, it's longing to just be there with Keith. She wanted to ask questions about his life and, most of all, to know how he was feeling. Janie had never felt anything like this before. She was actually quite surprised by the power of what she assumed first love could do.

She sped up and caught up with Keith and Vanessa and did her best to forget about the feeling she was having.

It took about ten minutes to cross Peck Park, which started a couple of blocks from the cemetery. Heading up the ramp for the overpass over the Long Island Expressway, they paused for a quick break in the middle of the overpass and watched the cars heading toward New York City. The stretch of highway was pretty straight, and even though the city was over ten miles away, on a clear day one could still see parts of the skyline. You wouldn't see much, just the really tall buildings, but it was still enough to make you feel part of the city, even if it was a distant part.

The other end of the overpass ramp led straight to St. Peter's High School, and the start of the Old Motor Way. St. Peter's Prep was known as the best school in the area. It was also the high school that Janie really wanted to attend, but Vanessa had pleaded with her to stay at BA for her high school years. Janie glanced at the school and then at the person who talked her out of it. Lastly she glanced at the boy who might make her forget about St. Peter's once and for all.

The Old Motor Way was actually just that. It was one of the first motorways, and private roads ever built for cars only. It was William Vanderbilt's personal road for him and others to drive to his summer house on Long Island. He also used it to have car races, until too many people got hurt in accidents.
 Some parts of the motorway were still used as roads while other parts had been turned into walking and bike trails.

The entrance to the roadway was the start and end point of the bike tour.

When Keith and the girls got to the site they saw two school busses and a rented truck just arriving. There were about eight or nine other kids and some parents that had arrived by themselves and were waiting.

Biking over to the busses they saw that Amanda was the first to step off the bus, dressed in a riding type light blue outfit. Kristen was right behind her in a bright orange sweat suit.

"Tom, will you get off the bus," Amanda yelled back inside the bus to her boyfriend. "You have to help me get my bike."

Janie's phone began to ring, reminding her that she had forgotten to call her mom.

"Yes, Mom," Janie said into the phone. "I just got here; I was just about to call. Let me go, we are going to start soon." She closed the phone quickly and put it back in her pocket.

It took about fifteen minutes for all the bikes to be unloaded and identified. All the people were required to stay in groups of twelve kids with one chaperone for each group. They were given colored rider identifiers which also had a giant letter representing their group. As they put on the giant red A's, both Kristen and Janie got disgusted how it clashed with their orange.

"One has to be prepared for the unknown," Amanda reprimanded Kristen. "Blue goes with anything," she said, as she used her hand to display her clothing choice.

At the last minute, Janie was allowed into Amanda's group because of a cancelation, though Janie could never really figure out who cancelled. Group A (for Amanda she pointed out included the P&P's, Janie, Keith, Dave and three of the boys on the baseball team as well the other three girls on the cheer and pep squad. Ms. Freeman was the chaperon. Janie found it weird seeing her and some of the other teachers outside of school, especially in riding gear which in case of Ms. Freeman was composed of bike pants, a yellowish shirt, wrap around shades and a very sleek looking helmet. You would almost have thought she was the leader at the Tour De France the way she was dressed.

"Wow, I didn't take you for a riding fan," Keith said to Ms. Freeman.

Janie was a bit annoyed hearing Keith's loose use of the word "Wow," but when she did a closer inspection of Ms. Freeman, Janie realized that the "WOW" was appropriate.

"Yes, Mr. Jackal, I am a riding enthusiast, and I have news for you." Ms. Freeman pedaled into the middle of the group. "See, they put me in charge of the A group because they want me to push this group along as fast as possible to prevent log jams. So I hope you guys all got a good rest last night because I am going to run you ragged."

Principal Chambers drove a little pink kid's bike to the front of the group and everyone started laughing. He blew a short blast from a foghorn can and grabbed the megaphone wrapped around his shoulder. He turned it on and played with the volume to minimize the feedback. "Okay, we have a few rules before we can start."

Soon the biking was under way and Jennifer Freeman had not been lying, as she forced a very steady fast pace for team A. Ms. Freeman would start at the front of the group, and then every once in a while coast to the back of the pack. The path was well cropped with trees on both sides, and occasionally they would come upon overpasses that allowed them over the roads below.

Ms. Freeman would frequently point out to Keith things on the trail, asking if they had those in California. Keith wasn't sure if she was joking or serious, so he would just answer "yes," if he knew. At one particular steep overpass, she pointed out to the entire class that this particular overpass was the first bridge made to allow cars to drive above other cars.

Keith started riding between Janie and Vanessa to keep away from Ms. Freeman's constant questioning. Kristin had tried to wedge her way next to Keith but after a while gave up and had started to ride with Tom's fellow ball mates.

"So how long have you been drawing?" Janie asked Keith.

"I don't know, forever." Keith's response gave Janie the feeling that, like her, Keith really didn't know exactly when he took up art.

"Me too," Janie smiled. "Usually girls and fashions."

"Me to," Keith said and they both laughed. "Actually, I like to paint the sea. You know, breaking against the rocks. Ships and birds fighting in the wind with the breakers right below them."

"So tell us about surfing," Vanessa interrupted.

"It's the greatest thing ever. Letting the ocean carry you. Putting your life in its hands, experiencing the danger and feeling the sea's power."

"The sharks," Janie talked over Keith's next description.

"Yeah, we don't talk about the sharks, it is their turf, we're just visitors enjoying the ride. We show the beasts the respect they deserve."

"So you've never been bit?" Vanessa jumped in, wanting to stay part of the conversation.

"Not by a shark." Keith winked a coy smirk, trying to add to the mystery of what things have nibbled on him.

"So what sports do they do in Flushing, Queens?" Keith asked with a sarcastic tone. "Tennis?"

"Janie and I are on the volleyball team," Vanessa said pulling her bike closer and wedging out Kristen, who was trying to work her way by Keith.

"Volleyball shouldn't be played in teams, just pairs. You guys probably don't even use sand," Keith said, still in a sarcastic tone.

"Heaven forbid; sand, it would get everywhere," Vanessa said sternly.

"Ain't nothing wrong with that. You end the game with a dip in the ocean. At least there are no floor burns. I will tell you what. You can pick my partner, and we will whip the two of you on a real volleyball court. There must be a beach somewhere around here. I mean, our school's town is called Bayside. I am assuming there is a bay somewhere, and that the bay has a beach."

Cunningham Park had something for almost any park enthusiast and it covered quite a bit of Flushing and Bayside. It has an environmental preserve, which the groups were just leaving, as well as numerous soccer and baseball fields. The bike path they were on now ran along many of these until the park ended. From there the path started to work its way behind houses. Ms. Freeman yelled back to Keith, asking him if the houses in California looked similar and Keith responded that they did. Janie noticed some writing on the path that indicated they were half way through the path. Group A rode for another fifteen minutes, crossing over overpasses and waving to people who were working in their backyards. An occasional jogger would slow down and squeeze by all the bikers, and all the kids marveled at how long the uninterrupted path ran.

Finally the houses seemed to be fewer and they started to enter Alley Pond Park. There was a very steep decline where Ms. Freeman took the lead and forced the group to slow down. Around the path it grew very wooded until it suddenly broke open into a large group of ball fields with a giant tennis bubble not too far off ahead of them. The bubble was so long that, if passing it on the Northern State Parkway, which is raised quite a bit over the park, it looked like a giant caterpillar about to attack Creedemoor hospital. The raised parkway, tennis bubble and the tall twin buildings of Creedmoor almost left you with the feeling that you were in a valley.

Group A had gotten quite a bit in front of Group B, and Ms. Freeman had gathered them into a fast clip. Reaching the half way point of the trip, the plan was for them to circle the ball fields and tennis bubble. This would allow all the other groups to exit the Old Motor Way before Group A re-entered it. Right across the street from the park area was Creedmoor Hospital. It was one of the most famous and notorious locations in the area because of it being one of the country's most famous hospitals for the mentally ill. The large yellow brick building with cages on all its windows was drawing stares from almost all of Group A. Even their teacher was staring across the road looking for someone fishing in a puddle or walking an imaginary dog. This fascination allowed a lone rider to go completely unnoticed as he headed from another trail and snuck into the pack. The Asian boy was racing toward the front of the group. He jumped off the path and kicked up some dirt as he pedaled past the riders and scooted in with the leaders of the group. Forcing himself in between Janie and Keith, a little out of breath, he excitedly said to Janie, "I figured out how to prove it."

Before Janie could get off any response, Vanessa yelled, "Bobby, did they let you out of the hospital for good behavior?"

"Very funny!" Bobby panted.

Vanessa continued her barrage, "Bobby, do you play tennis?"

"No, they don't let me anymore; I hurt myself too many times."

Before Keith could ask how someone could hurt himself repeatedly playing tennis, Vanessa chuckled and said, "Keith, I think we found your volleyball partner."

"Janie, I figured out what we are going to do; we need to go to Washington. We can get the ultimate answer. What did Lee Harvey Oswald know?"

"The person who shot Kennedy?" Keith inquired.

"Did you know that John Kennedy was a captain in the army?" Vanessa added.

"I thought he was in the navy," Keith said.

"He was," Bobby answered. "Who is this?" Bobby asked Janie.

"Bobby Wu, meet Keith Jackal," Janie said over the confusion.

"Jackal," Bobby repeated Keith's last name.

''Wu." Keith nodded a hello in return as he stopped pedaling and coasted for a moment.

"I am sorry. I was actually confirming that you were named after a wild canine from Africa," Bobby said.

"OH! Well, that's me. So what's a Wu?"

"It was an ancient province of China," Bobby stated matter of factly. Knowing the true matter of fact was Wu did not sound as impressive as Jackal.

"Well, it looks like we are going to be sharing signals, so are you a setter or a striker?" Keith said to his chosen volleyball partner.

"I think I will need to research that," Bobby retorted as they continued down the path.

With Creedmoor moving out of Group A's line of sight, Bobby had now taken on most of the conversation. Ms. Freeman, like an experienced biker in the Tour De France, started working her way through the pack.

"Janie, I figured out what we can do, but we have to do it quickly," Bobby said getting back to his original conversation.

"Bobby, you are not supposed to be here, you're going to get me in trouble."

"Alright, just make sure you call me tonight. We have to make preparations,"
Bobby said as he rose off his seat and started to put his bike in overdrive.

Ms. Freeman worked her way up to Janie and the others, as Bobby was beginning to pull away. "What is going on here, who is that boy?" Ms. Freeman inquired, not the least out of breath from her sudden move to the front.

The girls remained silent. Keith watched until Bobby was a good distance away. He finally moved a little over, letting Ms. Freeman move to the head of the pack with him, as he said, "I don't know, Ms. Freeman, but he was talking what seemed to be a whole bunch of mumbled jiberish. He's too far away to catch now though."

"Oh yeah!" Ms. Freeman said. In a second she lunged a bike length in front of the students stating, "As we say in biking, watch me chase this rabbit down."

Ms. Freeman never raised off her seat but started to exert great force with each push of the pedals, and within only fifteen seconds she was half way between the group and Bobby.

In the meantime another change to the lead pack was happening as Kristen tried to wedge her way into the vacant gap left by Ms. Freeman's break to chase down Bobby. Vanessa tried to close the hole, and her front wheel touched with Kristen. Both girls went flying off their bikes, with Vanessa landing in the dirt with Kristen landing beside her with her left knee scraping on the hard tar surface of the trail.

Ms. Freeman was just about at Bobby's back wheel when she heard the screaming behind her. Looking over her shoulders and seeing the entire group stopped, she gave up chase of Bobby and returned to Group Amanda.

Most of the bikes were laying on the ground and everybody was tending to Kristen.

The cut wasn't that bad but Ms. Freeman said that it would not be a good idea to ride with it. Keith offered to race back to his car, so he could pick up Kristen and her bike. As the other groups arrived, they all decided that Keith was the quickest way to get a car there. One of the chaperones stayed with Kristen and another went with Keith as he raced off to retrieve his car. The entire class, which had become one large group now, set off on the last leg of the last Bay Academy Bike rally together. They all chanted "Kristen" and yelled inspiration to her as they headed back to the Old Motor Way.

Riding without boy

51

"I bet you she scraped her knee on purpose," was all Vanessa kept saying as she and Janie rode home without Keith. The ride home from the bikeathon seemed longer than the original trek there. The trek home was most definitely more uphill and the girls had been biking for over three hours now, but what really seemed to make the trip less enjoyable to both was the lack of Keith.

"He probably went to First Care Medical Center with her. Now they're going to have that connection, all because her knee hit the pavement. Why, Why couldn't it be me?" Vanessa cried.

"Vanessa, you are being an idiot. Besides, maybe you can call him later and tell him you got a case of whiplash when you flipped over his car."

"Talking about idiots, what the heck was Bobby talking about?" asked Vanessa, moving the conversation away from her hands free riding experience.

They finally reached the cemetery, but the back gates were already closed so they rode on the dirt that was between the road and the cemetery wall. It was a little bumpy and it made Janie's voice tremble as she replied, "Who ever knows what that boy is talking about."

"Why was he saying you should see Oswald? Isn't he dead?"

"Oh, it's just some documentary he wants me to watch. Hey, look over there." Janie said, pointing into the cemetery, "There always people at that tombstone. You see them, right?" Janie quizzed Vanessa about the strange area where she always noticed people congregating.

"See who? I don't see anybody," Vanessa replied.

"You don't see them?" Janie said, full of surprise.

"Of course I see them. What, do you think they are ghosts or something?" Vanessa chuckled.

"No, it's just.. Why are there always people there?"

"Maybe the person had a lot of family, or maybe there's some great secret they are trying to find out, you know like buried treasure or something," Vanessa replied, hoping to put an end to the pointless conversation.

The girls reached the corner, which was actually a pretty high climb up hill. You wouldn't call Flushing another San Francisco, but it has its share of hills, and some can take the breath out of you on a mountain bike.

As they started coasting, Janie's phone beeped that she had received a text. She took her phone out with one hand and flipped it open. It was Bobby.

"Who is it?"

"Bobby, he texted me "Jan". The boy could build a cold fusion device but he can't figure out how to text a full message. He always sends only part of what he is trying to write by mistake. Then it takes him another fifteen minutes to retype the rest."

"Aren't you going to reply?" Vanessa said inquisitively.

Janie put her phone back in her pocket and cheerfully said, "No, it will just confuse him. I'll wait."

After a long day of biking, both girls milked the coasting as long as they could, until both bikes were about at a crawl a block from Janie's house. They hugged and pedaled in different directions to their houses.

Janie burst through the kitchen door, and before her mother could ask her about the trip, Janie told her all about the motor way and the big accident. Janie's excitement almost caused her mom to forget, but as Janie was leaving the kitchen her mom yelled out, "Honey, I found this under the seat in my car. Funny, I thought you hadn't been in the car for weeks," her mom said, a little confused as she handed Janie her house keys.

"No, I went in it this morning looking for the garage key," Janie replied, quickly enough to end any suspicions by her mother.

"Oh, us and keys just don't work well."

"Yeah we should just leave everything unlocked," Janie quipped. "Or get punch pad or eye scan thingies."

"Your father won't spring for a new sofa, I don't think he will be up for that," Janie's mom said with a bit of sarcasm.

Janie ran up the stairs, flipped open her phone, and read her second text from Bobby.

*Janie IM me when you get home

It took him five minutes to type that she thought as she fired up her computer and logged on to AIM. Well actually first she checked the top 100 hundred on iTunes. "How is

'Blah Blah Blah' still in the Top Ten, it's the complete waste of a spot."

About two seconds after Janie had finished turning AIM on Bobby flashed her a message.

*Bobby: Janie so how is the top ten
**Janie: BlahBlahBlah is still there
*Bobby: Its not that bad
**Janie: W/E
**Janie: Hey what were u doing today
*Bobby: I had to talk to you I figured out what we need to do
**Janie: And what would that be??
*Bobby: You shut off the AIM recorder your dad activated
**Janie: Yeah its turned off right now
*Bobby: Gd I searched a couple of unknown solved secrets carried to the grave like Houdini, and this tree guy
**Janie: Tree guy??
*Bobby: Yeah he made really cool trees, nobody knows how he did it, Axel Erlandson and the tree circus it was called
**Janie: Sounds pretty lame.
*Bobby: No they are ridiculous google tree circus
*Bobby: I don't think he would tell us anyway or we would understand it
**Janie: Would we want to know, I like Houdini
*Bobby: Yeah, he's right here in Brooklyn too but his wife blabbed the secret.
**Janie: What secret
*Bobby: The code he left for someone to retrieve from him in the afterlife.
It went *Rosabelle answer tell pray answer look tell*
But she told someone and it got out.
**Janie: Well then what

*Bobby: Oswalt there is no greater mystery than if he was the lone gunner.

**Janie: The grassy knoll.

*Bobby: Yes the grassy knoll and was he aided by the communist or the Mafia

**Janie: So you think he will tell?

*Bobby: Well he never got the chance to speak maybe he wanted to and never got the chance

**Janie: And we will just go there and ask him

*Bobby: That's what I was thinking

**Janie: And where is there

*Bobby: Washington

**Janie: I don't think my student bus pass will take me that far.

*Bobby: No but the $200 Mrs. Mabbit gave you will get us there and back.

*Bobby: We can do it in 9 hrs. That's why we need to do it one of the days after Tuesday when spring break begins

**Janie: Are you serious?

*Bobby: WAY serious

**Janie: So what day

*Bobby: WTF You pick

**Janie: Don't you WTF me.!! You pick

*Bobby: Okay T

**J: T?

*Bobby: Thursday

**Janie: OH!!!!

*Bobby: Yes

*Bobby: Yeah we are both off we will both claim to be going to the others house.

**Janie: What if they call?

*Bobby: Have they ever called??

**Janie: There is always a first

*Bobby: Well then well just stay in Washington, run for Congress

**Janie: GTG Call you tomorrow.

Janie took one more look at the top 100 just to make sure it hadn't changed, shut her computer, and fell back onto her bed. The bike trip had worn her out, but the conversation with Bobby had filled her with enough energetic thoughts to not allow her to fall right asleep.

Looking out her window there were no lights in the cemetery, and the moon was barely a sliver. Although the street lamp about a half block away was on, it didn't really light the cemetery at all. Janie just stared out into the darkness. Occasionally she would see a flash of redirected car headlight against a polished tombstone.
She just kept staring, thinking about the possible trip, what if they really contacted him?
The day had been so long, so much happened, Bobby, the plan, yet what she saw most when she stared into the darkness was visions of Keith, laughing and smiling as he drew and surfed and then rode his bike up close enough to her window to kiss her goodnight as she fell asleep.

Viva La France

Vanessa was on the bus Monday morning, and the first thing out of her mouth was how she was sure that Kristen scraped her knee on purpose. Janie started studying French feverishly. "What is the verb for fly?" Janie asked, looking through the vocabulary section.

Vanessa nonchalantly opened her left hand and searched her fingers to see if she had written that one down. "Will the proper noun for boat work?"

"No!" Janie said, as she continued through her book.

"Well then," Vanessa said, as she opened and then read from her other hand, "Je Ne Sais Pas."

"Huh." Janie looked up as if an if she had just been addressed by the bus driver. "Did you just say I don't know in French?"

"Yes, I plan to use it for at least two or three answers on the quarterly today."

"Did you ever think it might be easier and less time to study than to devise ways to pass without studying?"

"The skills I am learning will be much more important to me than the French you will have forgotten by the time you graduate college."

"The scary part is you might be right."

Vanessa opened her left hand and refocused her eyes to it. "Veritas vos liberabit," Vanessa said in almost the correct Latin phrasing.

"I don't even think that's French," Janie said, giving up and going back to her studying.

With a look of panic Vanessa exclaimed, "I was taking random sentences off the internet. I must have picked a couple of other languages." Vanessa opened her hand one more time and exclaimed "Zut Alors!"

The bus dropped the students off about a block away from the school. The walk was a nice break from studying for both of them. Vanessa's mind wandered away from France and back to Kristen. "I swear if that leg is not broken, I am going to break it."

They bolted up to homeroom. There was Kristen with a short enough skirt to discreetly show off her wrapped knee; Keith sitting in his seat behind her.

"Kristen, oh I was so concerned. Are you alright, deary?" Vanessa said with such sincerity that Janie began to wonder if she meant it. "We are all so lucky we have Keith here to watch over us," as she looked softly at Keith.

"V, J," Keith said, "you girls ready for the French test?".

Vanessa opened her hand and said, "Une vache ne devrait pas monter une bicyclette."
Finishing with a smirk she walked to her desk.

"Ni si un faon jaloux devrait parler le français," Keith said as he turned and watched Vanessa and Janie take their seats. Neither girl seemed to hear or understand Keith's little snip.

Every free second up to the actual test Janie spent looking up words she did not remember. The only word she never found, fly, was the second vocabulary word on the test. It was the only question she missed. Janie handled the listening and essay parts perfectly. Her lack to get of the ground and fly in French left one possible score that could better hers.

Roll Call

Mrs. Kaya was an elderly Indian lady who was one of the last people you think would be a French teacher, but sometime looks can be quite deceiving when it comes to languages. She was also the hardest tester in the school. Her French test scores could go as low as the 50's and often the a class average would be in the low 70's. She didn't curve the grade either but would allow extra credit. Sometimes kids would have to submit over ten extra credit projects just not to have summer school. One of the great things about being a language teacher was you didn't have as many classes as some of the other teachers and this allowed Mrs. Kaya to report back to the troops bright and early on Tuesday on the success or failures of their mission.

As she started to read the test scores that dark Tuesday morning, it wasn't sounding good for the class. That was until Mrs. Kaya got to Janie. Her voice filled with pride as she said, "Now for one of my star pupils to save the day, Janie Kelly with a quatre vingt dix huit. That's ninety eight to all you lay people."

Janie headed to get her test score wondering what Mrs Kaya meant by one of her star pupils. Janie always thought she was the only star in Mrs. Kaya's eyes. Janie was pretty confident if the class bus broke down in Paris without Mrs. Kaya, she was their only prayer.

Her confusion was soon cleared when Mrs. Kaya called up Keith. "Mr. Jackal, I am not sure how good the school system is in California, but your French teacher must have been maginifique," Mrs. Kaya said, as she raised her hand with Keith's test and went on about the 100 he got.

The last test Mrs. Kaya called was Vanessa. Vannessa pumped her fist as Mrs Kaya announced a 66. "It is quite amazing," Mrs. Kaya went on, "knowing that over 65 is passing that you could somehow factor to do exactly enough to get you a 66 every time. It is simply amazing, not to mention a little satanic," she joked.

"Veritas vos liberabit," Vanessa said as she took the test from Mrs. Kaya.

"The truth shall set you free." Mrs. Kaya, who also knew a great deal of Latin, translated.

"Yes, that too," Vanessa replied, not realizing that Mrs. Kaya was translating.

The rest of the day Janie squirmed in her seat. Occasionally she would look at Keith; Keith often nodded when he saw Janie looking in his direction. Janie's stare was not filled with anger, but yet anger was part of it. There was also confusion, as she tried to figure out if Keith knew what he was doing, what craziness he was causing. Janie also realized on one particular stare that there was also another reason. He just looked so hot in that shirt. Janie found another reason to sneak additional peeks as she decided that a future fashion designer studying a shirt and the way it fits someone is something that she needed to study in detail. And today, yes today, was a good day to start.

The bell rang for the last time of the day, releasing all the students from their daily sentence. Janie took one more stare at Keith while he was rising out of his chair. She grabbed her bag and headed to the gym for practice.

Vanessa had caught up with her about halfway to the gym. "You going to be able to play today?" Vanessa asked Janie.

"Huh?" Janie responded not understanding Vanessa's interruption.

"You know, with the way you kept twisting your neck to check out Keith too, I just figure you might be too sore to play," Vanessa quipped.

Janie went to hit something in front of her. There was nothing to hit but she hit it hard anyway. Was the staring that obvious? she thought. All those times he nodded he was probably just laughing at the poor doe-eyed school girl, she thought, getting madder each second till finally she roared, "That boy is trouble. He might not look like it, but he is trouble."

"Well, you're going to have trouble if you get in my way," Vanessa said very matter of factly.

The volleyballs at practice took a savage beating as the full squad of eight girls went through their usual serving drill. After Kristen made sure to double check that no one aside from her teammates was present she stopped her dramatic limping and started the barrage. Her practice serves got harder and harder as she overheard Vanessa on the other side of the net mentioning how maybe some kids should have never taken their training wheels off. Vanessa was in a front position but she needn't be too nervous of being hit because as Kristen got madder her serve got wider. Her last shot caught the pole of the net with such force it caused the weighted stand to wobble back a good six inches. The ball bounced back toward Kristen who picked it up as Ms. Hill blew her whistle.

"Vanessa you're up," said the coach as she stared at Kristen, surprised by her lack of concentration. As she passed by Kristen, she took the ball and slammed it into Vanessa's chest yelling, "Well at least I only need training wheels!"

Vanessa almost dropped the ball and lunged at Kristen, but quickly decided that it would be better and safer to show her up on the court. As she got to the serving line she saw Kristen in the middle of the opposing side of the court. Her back was to Vanessa as she was chatting it up with Bridget about the zinger she just laid on Vanessa. The freckles on Vanessa face had started reddening and expanding till they looked as if they might start to explode all over her face. Vanessa threw the ball a little in front of her with spin so that it came back and just as it did she lept into her serve. Like a bullet it hit Kristen in her back as she continued her talk with Bridget the captain about her remark.

Kristen turned and started to bolt under the net as Coach Hill jumped in between the girls. She almost swallowed her whistle as she attempedt to break up the altercation. Things finally started to settle down as Vanessa was escorted by Ms. Hill to the service area to finish her practice serves.

The anger being taken out on the poor volleyball didn't stop there though, as coach called the last starter, Janie, to the line to hit her serves. All day Janie had been getting angrier and angrier about Keith coming in here and throwing everything into disorder. That cute little smug face. "I Want to smack it!" she yelled to herself as she bounced the ball hard on the floor. Yelling in her head, "Where does he come off getting a 100," as she leaped into the air and riffled a serve. Vanessa and Kristen both in the front and wanting to both show off at the net, jumped in unison to block the serve, but the force of Janie's shot blasted through both of their blocks, hitting the back line before slamming into the gym door. As the two descended they looked at each other and remembered that in the gym they are a team. They also both took a quick look at Janie or "CG" as she was getting to be known and realized that outside the gym she might be trouble.

Kristen's sympathetic limp immediately returned upon her exiting of the gym. She yelled, "Will you please be careful!" at Janie and Vanessa as they rushed past her. Janie and Vanessa caught the Q31 bus that they were racing to the bus stop.

"I told you that limp was fake," Vanessa said as they found two seats together. Janie hated taking the bus home from volleyball as it was always crowded with people heading home from work.

Janie had noticed the bus driver was a pot stirrer. Pot stirrer was Janie's nickname for drivers who adjusted the driving wheel so it was like the top of a cauldron, and then would turn the wheel as if they were a witch stirring a pot. Janie never felt comfortable with pot stirrers for it did not seem a natural way to drive.

"Maybe she limbered up during stretching," Janie replied, knowing it was not the case but keeping true with the Rebel's code of what happens in practice stays in the gym.

"Whatever," Vanessa said, giving up her rant. "So what are you doing for break? Are we going to hang?"

"After Friday, I have some things planned with the family. I think Thursday we are taking a ride up to Ossining to visit my Aunt Joan," Janie said in a nervous tone that Vanessa did not pick up on.

"Nice."

"My father is giving me hell about my minutes lately so don't call me Thursday or Friday. I might be in the car and I know he is going to give me a lecture every time the phone rings."

"So I asked Keith if he would mind helping me with my French studies," Vanessa said quickly hoping to not dwell on her not asking Janie.

"I'd be insulted if I didn't know you don't really study French." Janie smirked. Her smirk hid the fact that she was actually insulted that she wasn't asked. What it hid even more than that was Janie's concern that Vanessa was starting her moves on Keith. Janie was still not sure if she wanted to hit or kiss Keith, but she was sure she knew what Vanessa wanted to do.

The Keith fever died down and by the end of the ride the girls had forgotten their possible adversarial roles and had gone back to small talk about classmates and the current top 40. Janie was careful not to slip up about her planned trip to Washington with Bobby. As usual she jumped off the bus at Dominique's Market after giving Vanessa a big hug and assuring her that they would hang out on Saturday or Sunday.

By the time she made it to the cemetery Janie could smell the flowers that were in full bloom. Janie loved flowers although a few gave off aromas that for some reason Janie never fell in love with. The smell grew stronger and stronger as Janie got deeper into the cemetery, and she started to regret cutting through it.

As Janie had dinner with her family her mood would swing from good to bad. At the table she would try to call the food by their French name, and once sarcastically noted, that Keith in French could probably describe the entire table's contents. Her parents were relieved when Janie mentioned she was going to go the Bobby's house after dinner for a little while.

She slammed the front door pretty hard when her dad in an attempt to humor her said "Bon Voyage," as she was leaving.

Janie hadn't thought much about Keith and the French test at first when she reached Bobby's house but soon she started to obsess about it again. She would often interrupt Bobby as they worked in the Wu's backroom study planning their trip. "I thought I would get the first 100," Janie said for the third time to Bobby that day. She was so distracted that almost all of Bobby's plans were met with little protest. She did not even object as he told her tomorrow after school she needed to come to his house directly so they could go to the Greyhound ticket office in Long Island City. It would have been cheaper to buy online, but neither had a credit card to use. Janie was surprised to learn that they would be able to buy the tickets as long as they were both sixteen.

It Can Be Dark in the Morning?

Janie stood on the wrong side of Utopia Parkway as the sun was just arriving in the sky. Most Fridays you could find her loitering at the bus stop across the street kicking at the crack in the sidewalk. She had actually made it noticeably bigger since she had started months ago and was afraid someone was going to yell at her. Usually the sun would be on the other side of the street and almost fully in the sky and warming her face. Today it was at her back and barely awake itself. Janie looked the other way into the sky, and she noticed the moon had not yet completely departed.

Janie leaned over to her accomplice for the day and asked, "Is there something wrong with this picture?"

Bobby, already in schedule mode, looked at his watch and answered in an annoyed voice, "Yes this stupid bus must have broken down"

"Don't you worry, the Q31 is never late," Janie assured him. "At least on that side," she said pointing to the other side of Utopia.

"Well, that would be very reassuring if we were headed to Bay Academy!" Bobby's attitude had not changed and he glanced at his watch one more time before he finally heard the bus. The Q31 limped into the intersection of 42nd Avenue before turning to chug its way toward them. "Thank God, this should get us to the Port Authority by 8AM."

"Oh, are we taking a boat?" Jamie asked, falling into a fog of early morning day dream light talk.

"No, it's the bus station's name in New York," Bobby responded.

"It must confuse people terribly," Janie added as the bus pulled up. "I thought we were leaving from where we bought the tickets."

"I told you Monday that we catch the bus at the Port Authority." Bobby was still sensitive about the time it would take them to get to the station; this was coupled with the fact that he was anything but an early riser and he shot Janie a look that said he didn't want to talk for a while.

The bus was somewhat crowded and as they worked there way to the back of a two-seater, Janie stared at the sad faces of people who must have the early shift at work. Sensing Bobby's desire for silence, Janie took the window seat and watched the new scenery as it rolled by. The biggest part of the landscape, St. John's University, almost brought a comment from Janie, but when she turned to look at Bobby he had dozed off. Janie let him sleep to the end of the university then nudged him awake, realizing that everywhere she went today relied on Bobby staying awake.

Bobby awoke, startled, and quickly looked around to make sure they had not passed Hillside Avenue. Luckily they hadn't, as Janie had woke him just in time. Bobby was familiar with the way to the F train, which he took many times last summer with his dad.

"So I changed my mom's phone contact info for your mom. It is now directed to your phone. Did you do the same?" Bobby asked gently so no one else would hear. With each second he was getting sharper and sharper, he was getting to be more like the Bobby Janie liked.

"Yeah, and I checked my dad's phone; he doesn't have your folks' number," Janie whispered back.

"Neither does mine," Bobby added as he dialed a number. "Listen to this; don't answer your phone." He handed his phone to Janie just as her phone stopped ringing. She put it to her ear, an automated voice came up and said, "You reached," the phone paused, "Evelyn Kelly," in a womans voice, chimed in before the automated system said to leave a message. Janie thought it really did sound like a canned cell phone message. The ladies voice was close enough to her moms that Mrs. Wu would never figure it was not real.

70

By the time Janie was done listening to the message Bobby had signaled the bus to stop and grabbed their knapsack. Janie followed Bobby off the bus which stopped right in front of the subway entrance. Bobby glanced at the sign to make sure it allowed access to the city bound F train.

Bobby swiped Janie and then himself through the turnstile as they headed deeper under the ground to the subway tracks. The F Train was one of the few trains, that, even as far as they were from the city was still completely underground. Right as they reached the bottom of the step the train arrived. Bobby happily looked at his watch, confident that the quick arrival of the train assured they would make their bus to Washington.

It was still a little early for rush hour and Janie was able to get a seat, with Bobby standing right in front of her. "Well that was quick," he said, "unlike that stupid bus."

Bobby was now full of steam while Janie was beginning to fall back into her morning fog. She let out a big yawn, followed by a quicker one as she settled down to relax and enjoy the ride. By the third stop, "Parsons Blvd," she was squeezed into the corner and the train had taken on the aspects of a cattle car on the way to the big house.

Somebody close to Bobby snickered agreement when Bobby stated to Janie, "This really is the F Train."

"Yes, I heard it use to be the D-, but it continued to run late." Janie added for fun.

A voice from the herd yelled, "That's not why they call it the F Train."

Janie turned to face Bobby with a shocked look, and they both decided to be a little quieter the rest of the way. The quiet inside Janie;s head mixed with commotion all about started to raise some doubts inside of Janie. They continued to the city as the herd got bigger and their smells got stronger.

After suffering through an assortment of bad odors for quite sometime, they finally arrived at the Times Square Stop which was only a couple of blocks from the Port Authority. It was only about 7:30 and Bobby suggested they pop inside a Dunkin Donuts to grab something to eat. Janie's doubts about the trip continued to grow the entire time on line until finally as they stepped outside the donut shop she let loose. First was the crying then as Bobby grabbed her arm and braced her against a construction wall for support she yelled, "This is just crazy; this whole thing is just crazy. Have you and your brilliant mind thought of that Bobby?"

Bobby continued to grab her arm and support her. "There is only one way to prove this whole thing is crazy, but yes, I have thought that it might be. It also might be one of the most remarkable things to ever have happened."

Bobby looked around to see if anyone took note of the commotion. A few concerned people seemed to make sure that Bobby was not causing Janie's distress, but after they made that judgment, the screaming seemed to be perfectly acceptable and they would continue on their way to work.

"Janie, there are just too many signs. I would love it to be coincidence but right now, I think it is more than that, and we owe it to you to find out." As he finished talking he looked into her eyes, not to sell his point but out of true concern for Janie. He thought this was the best way to

72

prove Janie's power, but he was not going to force Janie to do it against her will.

"There have been a lot of coincidences," Janie nodded as she stopped sobbing.

"They are even happening now." Bobby had taken his eyes off of Janie and was looking behind her at the construction site wall.

"What do you mean?" Janie's confusion to Bobby's comment help ease her anxiety.

"Turn around," Bobby instructed Janie by pointing to a poster on the makeshift plywood wall.

Janie had not paid much attention to her surroundings since they left the electronics of Times Square, but as she turned around to look at the barrier she was amazed to see five of the same oak-tag sized poster that read "Dead Kennedys LIVE April 22 – 24". Under the initial heading was a crazy looking insignia and the location of the performance.

"Oh my God, it's tonight!" Janie said, allowing the strange circumstance to calm her nerves. "Want to see them on the way home?" she laughed.

"I never heard of them," Bobby said as he released her arm. "What a horrible name."

"Well, maybe we can help one of them rest a little easier, and I think we should do our best to do that," she said with a renewed confidence.

The bus was twenty minutes from pulling out when they got on. They grabbed seats near the back of the bus. The bathroom was in the back on the same side with its door adjacent to the back row. The travel to the bus, coupled with their early rise, had worn them both out a bit as they both rested heads on each other. Janie laid her head on Bobby's shoulder as Bobby rested his head atop Janie's head. Bobby had never been in this position before; he had thought about it, however, it had just never happened before. Suddenly, Bobby realized that this ride might bring them closer in a particular way than they had never been. Bobby was not upset with this thought at all.

Janie's hair was tied in the back in a bun kind of form, even pulled back her brown hair was so thick and springy. Bobby rested his head on it and found it quite pillow like. He even tried to fluff it as a joke. When he did, he was quite surprised to see that he could not even feel her skull through the tightly pulled back hair.

Janie did not find Bobby fluffing of her hair humorous, and lifted up her head. The bus had filled up quickly, and was just about to leave. Bobby and Janie spent the rest of the time watching people enter the bus, including the driver, who was small and older for a bus driver, felt Janie. He was also pretty plump, however, Janie had seen many plump drivers on the Q31. She often thought the Q31 must be a desirable bus route for the plump driver because she could not ever remember a skinny one.

Most of the people had entered the bus and they were now staring at the back of many of their heads. An old lady with hair much like Mrs. Mabbit's was in the row in front of them. Janie told Bobbie this was another good omen. A man with a cowboy hat headed to an empty in the middle of the bus.

"He doesn't look like a cowboy," Janie said, leaning into Bobby. "But it's another good omen."

"It's definitely a good omen for me," Bobby said. "Remember, I bet a $1 that there would be somebody wearing a cowboy hat on the bus."

An elderly lady with long messy hair bundled in a rain coat came on board as Bobby and Janie were talking. She was struggling with her bag; behind her was the bus driver. "What in the world is in this bag?" he asked as he started to drag it down the aisle for her.

"Rocks!" the lady exclaimed. As the bus driver tossed the bag under the lady's seat, the bus actually shook a little. He walked back to the front of the bus muttering something about retirement. He grabbed a clipboard and walked down the aisle counting heads and then writing the number down. When he was done he signed the bottom of the document on the board as he said, "And away we go."

 The bus had a certain Frito smell, and Bobbie and Janie were now discreetly sniffing in people's direction attempting to figure out who was causing the smell. Bobbie was sure that it was coming from the bag of the rock lady, but Janie disagreed. She was sure it was coming from the dude in the cowboy hat.

The bus driver announced the three stops the bus would be making, closed the door and threw the bus into gear. It wasn't more than five minutes till the first person headed to bathroom. Janie studied the person as he walked; he was a raccoon, she thought to herself. She pulled out her pad and started to etch him. Janie usually associated people she was going to draw with an animal. She would usually mix the features together in a way that the person wouldn't notice but she felt it gave each person a little more uniqueness.

"He's not the Frito maker but he is making quite his own stink." Janie whispered to Bobby.

Bobby was resting and opened his eyes.

"What you drawing?" Bobby asked.

"Oh nothing, I was just going to draw some of the people on the bus," Janie said as she sharpened and then used the pad sheet to re-dull her pencil to her likening.

"What about me? All these years we've been friends and you've never drawn me."

Janie started poking the paper like she was pricking something, as she told Bobby, "That's because after I draw a person, then I can control them like a voodoo doll."

"You couldn't control me. I have a superior intellect." Bobby raised his hand in the official superior intellect finger raise.

"Are you sure? I'll bet you that dollar I owe you. That after I draw you I could make you do whatever I say."

"Really, why don't you draw me?"

"Okay, but you can't get mad," Janie requested.

"Not unless you give me a third eye," joked Bobby.

"Actually, I was going to give you a second nose, so you could figure out where this Frito smell is coming from."

Janie peeled her pad to a new page. Took a careful look and started to draw, just as the bus entered the tunnel leading to New Jersey. They were about half way through New Jersey by the time Janie was done.

"Okay, close your eyes," Janie said

Bobby obliged and closed his eyes.

Janie laughed, "I think you owe me that dollar; I told you I could make you do whatever I say after I draw you."

Bobby tried to protest with his eyes still closed but soon agreed that they were back to even. "Well, let me see what I look like anyway."

"Open your eyes," Janie said, a little nervous.

"Nice, but why do I look like a bear?"

Crossing Washington

The bus let them off into the heart of Washington. The cemetery was cross town and Bobby knew they had to hurry. He had them run outside and down the block to the middle where the city line bus stops were. They jumped on the M40. The M40 would take them all the way to the gates of Quiet Grounds Cemetery. Bobby had estimated by its distance for it to be about a twenty minute bus ride. He, of course, had not estimated that crossing Washington in a vehicle was not something that could be measured by distance alone. No, there was an additional force that

Bobby had overlooked in his equation. Like Einstein Bobby quickly realized his mistake and scribbled on a piece of paper. "We've got a problem." Bobby stated looking up from his scribbled schedule.

"You didn't calculate for the traffic, did you?" Janie had a look that showed the long amount of uneasy traveling they had already been through.

"Who could calculate this? I mean Einstein was wrong. Space travel cannot stop time but Washington DC traffic, well darn it could stop just about anything I think."

Janie had changed her hairstyle back into the bun type style she had started the day with. It irritated Bobby who was feeling the stress of the time crunch. "Are you afraid we are being followed?" he asked sarcastically.

"What?" Janie asked, a little confused.

"Your hair, that's like the fifth time you changed styles. You're making me nervous."

Janie looked out the window and noticed the Jefferson Monument but it didn't quell her anger. "You don't know what its like! At least once a week somebody tells me how lucky I am. How they wished they had my hair, and you can't say OH No you don't. You just say thank you. Meanwhile this hair is so heavy I get tired just holding my head up sometimes. And it pulls on my scalp so much, that is why I am always rearranging my hair. Not to mention that I have tried every hair product from here to Morocco just to allow me to run a comb through it."

Bobby was both listening to Janie's tirade and looking out the window for Amber Street. He was relieved to spot it and pulled the signal rope quickly. The bus came to a quick stop and Bobby grabbed his knapsack and shuffled Janie off the bus. He was quite thankful to see that the sudden departure from the bus had distracted Janie from her rant.

Bobby looked at his watch, 2:12 was much later than he had anticipated. He knew they had to be back at the bus station by 4:45. He had them walk at a pace, just under a jog. It was two blocks down Amber until they would hit Quiet Ground Cemetery. Janie was walking closer to the street and admiring the Cherry Blossoms that were in bloom. They were not everywhere like she had seen on some of the streets on the bus, yet they were quite beautiful and they helped Janie's overall nervousness calm down quite a bit.

At the pace they were walking, the two blocks took no time. The cemetery was gated with the usual black cast iron fence. It was at least another block to the entrance gates. Janie continued to look at the blossoming trees, while Bobby had been taken to staring into the cemetery as they walked. They were walking so fast that as Bobby stared into the cemetery the fence started to make him feel like he was looking at an old movie reel. The picture had that same choppy feeling to it. He immediately thought of the assassination film that he had watched over and over again in the last weeks. The slowed down version, then seeing it sped up, the version with added audio. Bobby had watched so many shows on the events of that day that he had drawn his own conclusion of what he felt happened.

Bobby was confident that there was no second shooter and did not plan to ask Oswald if there was. No Bobby planned to ask Oswald what he thought the real unanswered question. Was he working alone or was he part of some conspiracy. There were quite a few scenarios, and all had some kind of strong reasons to be possible.

It was close to three by the time they finally got to the cemetery. Janie had taken over carrying the knapsack, and was searching through it to grab the last pack of Ding Dongs.

Bobby and Janie had not really thought about it until they reached the front of the cemetery but now they both commented on the lack of tombstones.

"From the pictures I saw I thought it might look like this." Bobby said as they stepped through the gates and past a small keeper's house. The cemetery or at least this part did not look like it was for the wealthy. The few tombstones that were there at all were very simple and so thin they almost looked that you could see through them.

A man looked out the window of the house and watched the two entering the cemetery taking the small road to the left. He knew where they were headed. He wasn't psychic or knew the reason why they were headed there, but he knew where they were going. He watched the same thing unfold almost everyday. Sometimes people would ask him where the grave was. He was not supposed to tell, but usually he would point them in the right way. If not the people would wander around for hours. But if you asked for Nick Beef well he would always send them the wrong way down the road on the right.

"Well, they must have been researching on the internet," he thought as he watched from the window the two disappear down the road to the west side of the cemetery.

As they continued down the road both of them were building with an unexplainable excitement. "Are you feeling it?" Bobby asked.

"Majorly," Janie replied. "I think my heart is about to jump out of my chest, though the scenery leaves a little to be desired."

"What do you mean?"

"Well I mean it's just that I was expecting more tombstones. This looks like Kissena Park.".

"Well, the people are buried here, and it's them we are trying to talk with, not their oversized tombstones."

"I know, it's just I was expecting a little more atmosphere," said Janie as she reached for her pocket. "Oh OH, just got a text."

"Is it…"

"Yep, it's mom," said Janie reading the text. "She wants to know if we rode King-da-ka yet." Kingda-Ka is the biggest coaster at Great Adventure and Janie had told her mom that they planned to ride it if the y had to wait two hours.. Her mom was very nervous about Janie riding it today, though if she knew Janie's real whereabouts, Kingda-Ka would seem much less stressful.

"Tell her no, that it was closed all morning," said Bobby, looking at his phone. "I was getting emails from a site that tells you if it's closed. The site says it's been closed most the morning."

Janie started to text as they stopped walking. She took more time than usual to send but mainly because she read it over just to make sure she did not slip up. She pressed send and looked at Bobby nervously.

"Well there it is." Bobby said as he pointed to a small tombstone.

Janie looked to where he was pointing, "Nick Beef, who is that?"

"That is another mystery taken to the grave site, only don't try to ask him because the grave is empty. They think it might have been a comedian and some routine he had only there doesn't really seem to be anything funny about it. What would be funny about being buried next to him?" Bobby asked as he pointed to the ground once more.

Janie's hairs tingled all over as she read the simple tombstone. Oswald was all it said. No first name, no dates, just Oswald. "I figured there would be something bigger, but now that I think about it; Why would there be? Oh Bobby, I am suddenly feeling very depressed."

"Hang in there Janie," Bobby said as he reached in the knapsack and pulled out a brand new drawing pad. He handed the pad to Janie who had retrieved a couple of artist pencils from her pocket. She looked around for a comfortable spot, but there was nothing around. There were no tombstones, no markers nor trees for a considerable distance. Janie asked for the knapsack as Bobby was getting a book of Sudoko puzzles.

"Why do you play those?" she asked. "Aren't they for the non-super genius?"

"No, Farmville is for the non super genius. These can be tough. I started doing math , crossword type puzzles but they were to easy. Plus, I need to do something that won't distract your channeling, and they worked in Calavery Cemetery so I figure I better stick with them."

"Superstitious?" Janie would be surprised had Bobby answered yes but she felt the need to make him admit he wasn't.

"I don't believe in superstitions but I thought you might," winked Bobby.

"So, are you going to ask the questions?" Janie inquired, as she used the knapsack for at least a little support for her back.

"I will try. Are you feeling anything?" Bobby inquired again.

"I am still feeling a little queasy from the bus ride, does that count?" Janie joked.

"No, it does not. Let me know when you are ready and I will start to concentrate."

Janie fixed the knapsack three or four more times and then called Bobby over. "I'm as ready as I will ever be," she said.

"Alright, let's gets going." Bobby started to concentrate and stare at the tombstone.
He had not told Janie the questions that he planned to ask. He did not want her own ideas to influence the outcome.

Janie sat there for a while bouncing the tip of the pencil against the paper almost like she was keeping beat. Twice she broke from the rhythm and looked as she was about to start sketching, but both times Janie just returned to tapping the paper. Bobby continued to concentrate on his question, till finally a third time, Janie broke from the beat, this time to start drawing.

Bobby continued to concentrate until Janie's drawing was well underway. As usual after a few minutes he went to work on a suduko puzzle but this time he barely got a quarter of the way through when Janie announced that she was done. Janie proudly lifted up her pad to reveal a very nice side view of what appeared to be JFK himself. Bobby studied the picture for some time before handing it back to Janie and announcing, "This is not good."

"What do you mean?" Janie answered, not completely sure if Bobby was insulting the quality of the picture or the drawing's relevance to Bobby's question.

"Well, I asked him who had helped him with the assassination. I do not think that our president helped in any way. I assume it is JFK." Bobby glanced at his watch.

"It looks like him," Janie said, confirming the likeness of the drawing to JFK.

"Let's try again," he said. Bobby again concentrated on the tomb marker and waited till Janie was deep into drawing before he started to work on a suduko.

Again when Janie was finished drawing a building, Bobby asked her his question. "What type of gun did he use?" seemed to have nothing to do with what she drew. A third drawing of the motorcade seemed to have nothing to do with Bobby's question on what was Lee's reason for shooting the President.

Earlier in the week Bobby had researched one person who was buried close to Oswald's grave. Bobby suggested they head over to the person's grave to see if Janie could connect with him. Sadly to the two, once again there seemed to be no link between the question that Bobby was asking the man and the drawing made at the site by Janie.

Neither Bobby nor Janie had expected this to happen. They both thought they would come down here and have no problem making contact. The entire day and lack of a successful communication with Oswald had started to wear on Janie. As they started to walk away from their last failure, she broke down crying.

"I thought I was special," she said as her crying intensified. "You know at first I thought it was just a fluke. But then I started to believe, and it felt good, you know, it felt like I was something important."

While continuing to head them toward the exit quickly, Bobby attempted to quell Janie's breakdown. "You are special," he said as he dragged her a little bit trying to kick start her walking.

"No I'm not," Janie sulked as she slowly began to move again.

"Yes you are." Bobby paused. "Janie. You are a great drawer, one of the top students in the class. You won so many academic and art awards."

"You know what I mean, my whole life I have stayed in the background, and never on the stage, just drawing the background scenes. I thought this was my chance to be on the stage." Janie slapped down her hands in frustration. "But it was all just a coincidence."

"It wasn't coincidence. Today kinda proves that, it just was not happening today. Now we have to figure out why," Bobby said, as if he was always applying scientific theories to the failure.

"Bobby, get over it. It was a coincidence. Its over!"

They had pretty much reached the front of the cemetery. The groundskeeper was watching them leave as they started to head for Amber Avenue.

The bus back to the terminal was even slower and by the time they got there Bobby's worst feelings had been realized. The bus had left over a half hour ago. He ran to the Greyhound counter, only to find out there were no available seats until tomorrow morning. He tried to reach other bus companies by phone but nothing seemed to be anybetter.

Janie had taken the news with blank stares. The most magical part of her life had just become a total train wreck, and nothing could clean it up. There was no knight in shining armor. Or was there? She suddenly thought.

"We should call Keith," Janie said in a tone that she hoped would not annoy Bobby.

"Jackal?"

"Yes, he has a car." Janie followed up her suggestion

"He is a surfer, great looking, and HE HAS A CAR," Bobby said annoyed.

"Will you get over it, he's our only hope." Janie interrupted the tantrum Bobby was having.

Seeing no other option, in a defeated tone, Bobby said, "Okay, call him."

Janie pulled out her cell phone and realized that her mom had texted a little while ago.

She started to text her back but made it quick so she could call Keith.

Say La Vie!

Vanessa moved a little closer to Keith. She stared into his eyes as he asked her again, "Le que et till?"

Vanessa looked at the clock in her room, pointed to the hands, she then looked back into Keith's eyes, "Je Ne Sais Pas."

Keith looked up at the ceiling. "You can't say you don't know for every answer. You pointed to the clock."

"But how do I know that it is working?" Vanessa asked, quickly pointing out, "I have not set it for weeks."

"Yes, I guess." Keith laughed and gave up. His phone rang as he was looking at his book for another question.

"Sacra bleu!" Keith said into the phone.

Vanessa got a very angry look on her face as Janie and Keith continued to talk.

"You need a what from where the both of you?" Keith exclaimed. "The state?"

"It's not a state," Janie said from the bus station.

"Actually, it is; you need to include DC in your statement, and I wouldn't put it past you to be calling from the state!"

"Really Keith, I need your help. You can't tell anyone, or Bobby and I will be grounded for life. Not anyone, promise"

"Okay, calm down. I will be there. Give me a couple of minutes and I will call you back when I am on the road," Keith said as the two ended their conversation.

Vanessa had been impatiently trying to figure out who Keith was talking to. But he had gotten off too abruptly for her to figure it out; all she knew was somebody was in Washington DC and in need of help. What was worse was; it seemed that Keith was about to come to the person's aid.

Keith had a nervous look on his face as he got off the phone. "I have some bad news," he said. "We will have to continue our studying tomorrow. A friend of mine called and needs a ride."

Vanessa tried to look as sad as possible, but it didn't help. Keith had to go to the bathroom before he left and Vanessa saw her chance. As Keith was in the other room she quickly grabbed his phone which he had left on the dinning room table.

Vanessa quickly found the received numbers area. She grabbed a pen and wrote half the digits down before she realized the number was Janie's. Vanessa quickly cancelled the menu and threw the phone back onto Keith's book a second before he came out of the bathroom.

"Vanessa, I gotta go, I don't know if you caught what I was talking about on the phone but a friend of mine needs a ride. We can pick this back up tomorrow night," he said as he grabbed his book and phone.

"And you were helping me out so much," she said as she glanced at her palm. "Merci Mon Capitan," she said as she brushed up against him to hug him goodbye.

As soon as Keith left, anger started to grow in Vanessa. She slammed the downstairs hallway door. She slammed the door at the top of the stairway, and the bathroom door on her way to her bedroom. Lastly, she slammed the bedroom door twice for good measure before grabbing her phone.

She thought about calling, then she thought about texting, then she realized if she accused Janie of anything Keith would know she checked his phone. She took a couple of deep breaths, and dialed Janie's number. Janie didn't answer and what was worse was it went straight into voice mail, which made Vanessa nervous that the two might be talking. She was a bout to try Keith again but thought this might lead to more suspicion about her snooping. So she followed up her call to Janie with an email.

Vanessa-: Where RU
Janie-: Home

Her response came quicker than she had planned and she assumed she was off the phone with Keith. She quickly decided to play along.

Vanessa: I'm going to come by
Janie: No
Vanessa: Y I got to vent
Janie: Sorry going out to eat
Vanessa: I will stop by just for a second
Janie: No walking out the door now going to dinner with the Wu's
Vanessa: OK TTYL
Janie: U2

The Wu's, Vanessa thought to herself. Of course, Janie never would have done this herself. She's too smart. This has Bobby written all over it. Janie is just too smart, however Bobby he is too smart for his own good, she thought. She opened her phone again and started to dial Janie's house. She stopped for a second and thought about the flood gates she was opening. But all she could see was Janie sitting in the front seat of Keith's car. Fixing her curly hair as Keith looked over at her. Vanessa finished dialing with the image still in her head, as she hit the send button.

"Oh, Hi Mrs. Kelly. I know you are about to go out to dinner with the Wu's. I just had a quick question for Janie and I think her phone was off."

The Hound of Quietville

Janie and Bobby made it back to the cemetery gates before 6:00pm closing. Janie was so nervous she was uncontrollably humming. They tried to go unnoticed as they reentered. Bobby led them to little group of bushes where they hid until the gates closed. Just a few minutes before, on the way back to the cemetery they both made sure to text messages to their parents close to the site where the demonstration was taking place. There was no way they were going to make it home in time. They knew the jig was up. So they both sent messages of their stupid plan to march in the protest, and how they missed their bus. They made up a story about luckily running into the older brother of a friend of Bobby's, who was driving them home when the rally ended. Both said their phones were on low battery, and they were going to turn them off for a while. Then Bobby had them both take the batteries out of their phones.

It was going to be at least four hours before Keith would sail to their rescue. While there was light, they decided to go back to Oswald's grave and try one more time; but it was to no avail. Bobby was sure that the drawings were in no way related to any of the questions he was asking. By about 8:20pm it was getting dark, and they decided that it was best to find somewhere to hang out in the darkness.

Janie and Bobby had made their way to the side of the cemetery where larger tombstones and mausoleums were allowed. The first few in the setting sky looked beautiful, but as time went on they started to get an eerier look to them. That together with the wind shaking the Cherry blossom into visions of swaying ghosts, Janie suddenly understood what Ichabod Crane must have been experiencing.

"Well, at least it's not Halloween," Janie said to Bobby, who was seeing if the front of a mausoleum door was loose.

"Would we really stay in there even if we were able to get in?" Janie asked as, surprisingly, the iron door creaked open.

"No, you're right, I was just curious. It looked like it was open," Bobby was saying as he pushed against the door and fell through into the darkness. Bobby, a little whiter and very embarrassed, leapt out of the mausoleum.

Janie laughed for the first time since being on the bus, as Bobby led them away from the mausoleum.

As they were walking away, Janie turned as she thought she heard something. "Did you hear that?" she asked Bobby, a little frightened by the sound.

"It's the wind," Bobby said, brushing off Janie's concern.

"You heard it?" Janie asked, half to make sure that she was not imagining things, and half to make sure that Bobby wasn't dismissing her question as her imagining things.

"No, but what else would it be? I am not sure if you noticed this Janie, but all the other people here are kind of dead, and not very talkative for that matter," Bobby added, referring to their failed medium attempts.

"Maybe it was an animal," Janie said, not allowing Bobby to dismiss it.

"This isn't the woods Janie; there are no lions, tigers or bears."

"What about really Big TOTO's like that one?" Janie said, as they came to a stop due to the large dog that had seemed to jump out from the darkness and cut them off from moving further down the path. The two went motionless as they contemplated the hair raising encounter. Bobby and Janie were not the only one's with raised hair.

"Okay, don't panic!" Bobby said.

"But, I'm scared he will sense it," Janie said, fully aware that animals sense emotions.

"Penn State did a study on that, it's not true," Bobby stated, as they both just stared at the dog in front of them. The mongrel seemed quite content for the time being to have a staring contest with the couple as well. "He seems to be wary of our talking as he seemed to stop advancing,.." Bobby continued.

"Well, I hope Fido read the study," Janie said, looking for stuff to say, "besides I do not think anyone in the study was as scared as I am right now; maybe there is a point where they can."

"Remember, we can communicate, and that is an advantage." he pointed out to Janie.

"Yes, and he can bite. I think that is a bigger advantage."

No one or beast had moved for quite some time. Janie was beginning to get antsy to move, but stood still as she could, and just continued to banter with Bobby, hoping it would keep the dog at bay.

Bobby took control of the situation and said to Janie, "Janie I want you to work your way to the side of the path, by the tombstone with the angel is a big broken branch."

The talking had stopped bothering the dog, and it again was advancing slowly as Janie also began to slowly move. The dog was black and brown and slightly thin, and as it slowly advanced toward Bobby, Janie noticed it had a limp. Neither the dog's limp nor its malnutrition made Janie comfortable that it was too weak to put up a fight. They both noticed that a majority, if not all of the dog's breed was German Shepherd, which didn't make either any more at ease.

With its attention purely fixed on Bobby, the dog did not take notice of Janie as she worked her way to the side of the tombstone. She grabbed the large broken branch with both hands, trying to be as quiet as possible.

Seeing Janie grip the branch, Bobby started to talk to the dog to keep its attention. "How fast is that doggie in the window," Bobby sang to the dog "The one with the crazed look in its eyes. How fast is that doggie in the window, Let's hope Bobby isn't SURPRISED."

"Take the branch and follow us NOW!" Bobby yelled as he tossed his knapsack at the dog and took off down the path. The dog dodged the bag and quickly followed Bobby down the path. Bobby made a beeline for the mausoleum, reaching it a second before the dog.

Inside the mausoleum, Bobby kept circling the casket with the dog barking right behind him. Quickly turning on the marble floor was allowing Bobby to stop losing ground and he actually had to slow down to not lap the dog.

Bobby saw that Janie had made it to the door, He instructed her to lunge with the branch when he exited the mausoleum. The timing was perfect; as Bobby leapt out Janie rushed to the door leading with the big branches leaves pointed at the dog. The obstruction caused the dog to stop pursuit and back up into the mausoleum long enough for Bobby to pull the door closed.

Bobby held his hand high on the iron gate like door, while Janie grabbed some braches and wedged them into the crack of the door. Bobby let go of the door and grabbed some more branches to use for wedges. He was still gathering additional branches as Janie headed over to the knapsack that Bobby had flung at the dog. She reached in and grabbed the remnants of Bobby's turkey sandwich, went to the gate, and tossed half of it to the dog.

"What are you doing? That's my sandwich," Bobby said.

"Well, this way if he gets out he will know we're friends."

"He also is more likely to try to find us now. Janie, I have no desire to adopt a rabid German Shepherd."

"But he looks so cute now." Janie made a lovey face to the dog. It finished and then looked up at Janie with big, round, dark, sad eyes.

"That's because he's in a cage. A tiger looks cute behind bars as well." Bobby jammed one more twig into the gap of the door.

Janie stopped listening to Bobby, and was making baby noises, as she threw the last piece of sandwich into the mausoleum. The dog watched Janie toss the sandwich and by time it hit the ground he had gobbled it up. He looked around the doorway, and with something in his tummy and in a nice safe crypt he lay down for a little nap.

"Janie, let's get away from these tall structures and head back to the area where Keith is going to meet us. There's a small bushy area there, and we can kind of keep lookout much easier there."

"Next time it might be a bear," Janie said. "You were very brave by the way; even if you were running away as fast as you could."

They headed over to the lower tombstone area of the cemetery constantly looking over their shoulder to make sure the dog had not escaped. By the time they got to the bushes it had gotten very dark. Janie pointed to Bobby in the distance; a man with a hand lantern was heading to the mausoleum's area that they just came from.

Janie and Bobby jumped into the bush area and hid. Bobby glanced at his compass wristwatch which had been helping them keep a good idea of where they were heading in the cemetery.

"Keith should be here within the hour. I think we should just lay low in this spot. Janie gave no argument. After seeing the way Bobby handled the dog situation, Janie would have followed any plan he came up with. Bobby heard her stomach rumble and said, "Bet you'd love a turkey sandwich right about now."

Who the Hell is Mrs. Valdez

Bobby and Janie were sitting pretty close to each other as they both tried to handle the nightmare of the last three hours. They had disconnected the batteries of their phones and attempted to forget about the Amber Alerts that were probably currently being sent through out New York. Janie joked to Bobby as to whose Amber Alert might be getting top billing. "You the one with the 100% average," she joked. "I am probably just a footnote, or maybe they are claiming that I kidnapped you."

"You did didn't you?" Bobby winked at Janie, but she couldn't even see his face.

"Hey I didn't come up with this stupid idea," Janie retorted.

"Well maybe if you could work your gift a little better, maybe we would be on the bus home with the wacky rock lady," pointed out Bobby.

"Oh this is my fault?" she asked with an annoyed tone.

Bobby went on, "Look this was my idea, my stupid idea, and I should have never talked you into this mess. I will

98

take all the blame. Maybe the fact that we were rallying for peace will save a little of my hide. I just hope they buy the rally thing."

Knowing that they left messages made them both feel a little more comfortable about the situation. It was close to ten o'clock and Janie turned her phone back on as Keith was supposed to call at ten on the dot. Hopefully, he was close to DC, Janie wished. Keith was more than close, only five blocks away just having pulled over to call them. Janie had been so cold, but felt a warmth come over her when Keith told her how close he was. They had been hiding in the cemetery since it closed at 6pm and Janie wanted out.

Keith's car pulled up out of the darkness and suddenly all of Janie's fear faded away. She wanted so badly to be home, no matter what the punishment, she did not care. She just wanted this entire chapter to be closed. No more trying to talk to dead people, no more cemeteries, just living things. She even looked forward to Mrs. Garret's history classes. What she looked forward to more than anything was being over these cemetery walls. It was as she was looking at the fence that she realized why Bobby wanted the rope.

Keith popped out of his car, checked his phone's GPS, and wondered why they were meeting at a desolate street in DC. He definitely was at the crossroads of Amber and Birch, but the place didn't seem too lively.

"PST," came a whisper that seemed to leap out of the cemetery.

Keith turned around. "I should have known this would end in a cemetery," he said. "Well, your hearse has arrived Madame."

"Enough with the satire," Bobby said, stepping into the small lighted area caused by Keith's headlights, "Where's the rope?"

Keith reached into his pocket and pulled out a ball of twine.

"WHAT!" Bobby yelled. "This is not rope."

Keith looked over at Janie and said. "You said 6ft of string."

"String rope; its kinda the same," Janie said in her own defense.

"No, No, it is not the same, rope and chain, that is the same. This couldn't hoist my pet dachshund over this fence. " Bobby kicked the ground knowing that this was going to add considerable time to their return.

"You got your dog here?" Keith jumped back in just for fun.

"No, I don't have my dog here," Bobby said not realizing Keith was joking.

"Well might I ask what you guys are doing locked in a cemetery anyway.

"I will tell you what they were doing," came a voice from the darkness within the cemetery. Everyone grew quiet as they looked into the darkness. "They came here to see the demon himself." The elderly Mr. Donovan turned on his lantern and stepped out of the bushes from where he had been listening to the conversation. He was still in his gray uniform and looked like a spectra as he stepped closer and continued, "Only there is nothing much to see just a tiny little tombstone with Oswald written on it."

"Hey, you were talking about Oswald the day of the bike trip," Keith said looking at Bobby in the now lit surroundings. "What, you got a thing about him?"

"You can't talk to the dead," the caretaker said. "I've seem a million people try, but they just ain't there. All you can do is cut the grass that grows over them. Now, why don't we all head down to the entrance, so I can let you kids out." Mr. Donovan motioned the way with his lantern and they all started walking.

"You're not going to bust us?" Bobby and Janie said in unison.

He shook his head at them then looked through the fence at Keith who was walking along the fence with them. "You are taking them home?"

"That is why I drove all the way here," Keith responded through the gates.

"Good they had a long day. I saw you guys come, go and then come back. I figured you had no place to go, and a cemetery is safer than the streets," said the man.

"That's what you think! That guard dog almost ripped us to threads," Bobby stated.

"There are no guard dogs," Mr. Donavan told Bobby.

"Well then, Mr. Mueller's long lost pet must have finally found his master," Bobby said. "They are happily sharing his mausoleum and a turkey sandwich right now."

Mr. Donavan grabbed his chin. "I thought I heard barking. That's why I came out here looking for the two of you."

They walked to the gate while Mr. Donavan pointed to some other areas in the graveyard, where other important people were buried but then finished with, "And all those great people rest here, yet the only one people come to see is a piece of crap murderer. Go figure."

Taking out his keys, Mr. Donovan unshackled the gates and then turned to Janie and Bobby and sternly said, "You won't mention me when you get home."

"No, No, of course not," Bobby said as the kids headed to Keith's car.

"Young lady," Mr. Donovan got Janie's attention. "You really should not come here this time of the year." Mr. Donovan turned and headed to the house like structure just inside the cemetery gates. He chuckled loudly as he headed back up its steps.

Janie had nodded acknowledgement to Mr. Donovan without really understanding his statement but as she headed to the car she thought more about it. Piling into the car, the seats felt like heaven to Janie and she stretched a little before totally relaxing.

"Guys, we have to stop somewhere for food. I am starving." Janie said.

Bobby murmured something about mentioning a turkey sandwich but quickly grew silent when Janie glared at him.

"I just passed a supermarket that was open," Keith said.

102

"Perfect, we will just grab something to go. Is it okay if we eat and drive?" Janie kind of pressed the stop on Keith, being very hungry and more than a little late.

"No problem," Keith said in his usual laid back way.

Janie was beginning to feel more herself every second, and once the car started moving the color started coming back to her face; a color that seemed to be fading more and more as the day had worn on.

They entered the supermarket and quickly made their way to the junk food aisle and Bobby grabbed a few bags of chips. Janie headed over to the cheese area, and after a while searching, finally settled on a wedge of Camembert. Keith grabbed two six packs of Pepsi and made himself a coffee with four sugars to help him stay alert.

At the checkout counter, Bobby paid using some of the money Janie got from Mrs. Mabbit. There was still plenty left, even after they used another $20 to fill Keith's gas tank. Before they left, Janie used the microwave at the front of the store to warm and soften her cheese. The first thing they did, returning to the car, was to turn on their phones and check message counts. Bobby had 32 messages and 12 texts. Janie had about the same messages but three times as many texts. Many were from Vanessa, who was writing in concern, but not letting on she knew anymore than what the Kelly's had told her which was not much.

Keith and Bobby were riding in the front at Janie's request. "So what do you think of what the caretaker said that I shouldn't go to the cemetery this time of the year. Why would he direct it at me? Do you think he knew something?"

After turning to quickly look at Janie, Keith reached and pulled the mirror off the sun visor, but before he could hand it to her Bobby caught his attention. He shook his head no but Keith not really understanding Bobby's protest, handed it to Janie. Bobby looked at Keith with an expression of impending horror.

Janie took the mirror and looked at herself. She went to brush the dust off the mirror that seemed to cover her hair in a lightish glow. Only the dust didn't seem to move when she swiped at it. She swiped at it a couple of more times before she patted her head. Touching her hair she could see a puff of pollen leap off her head. Bobby was watching with a tense feeling similar to watching a firework right before it goes off. The fuse was burnt down and you are just waiting for the bang. Bobby knew the firecracker was going off and realizing the countdown was at zero he cringed a little behind the headrest.

She patted her head again as it finally sank in. Janie looked around for Bobby's face, repositioned herself so the headrest was at an angle and locked onto Bobby's eyes.

"Why didn't you tell me?" She screamed. "You let me walk into the store looking like this?"

"Oh, what am I supposed to tell you? That you have some sort of magnetism to pollen. I tried to dust you off, but you almost took my head off." Bobby tried yelling louder. It was a cheap debating trick but often worked.

"Pull over!" Janie demanded.

"What?" the boys said in unison.

"Pull over! I have to fix this mess," Janie said as if there was no other option.

"First it's dark, second I am transporting fugitives, third, there are probably snakes on the side of the road." Keith did not bother to use his fingers to express the numbering as he was driving.

Giving in Janie said, "Well you are lucky there are snakes." After searching for a brush in her bag, Janie rolled down the window and sticking her head out and used the wind to brush free the seedlings and other vegetation from her hair.

It took her about two full minutes of brushing for Janie to feel that all the yuckiness had been removed. When she was done she put her hair into a bun syle.

"Hairstyle number eight," Bobby whispered to Keith.

"What did you say?" Janie said in a voice that let Bobby know he should not tell the truth.

"I said that I got a picture of you and me that Fitz from computer club doctored putting us at the United Rally for Peace."

"Great, did you send it to my phone?" Janie inquired forgetting about the hair comment..

Keith started to speak as Bobby showed the processed picture to Janie "There are no toll booths for quite a ways, at least until we get near the G. Washington Bridge, but from now on, could we try to be a little less noticeable. I brought a blanket and you guys will have to lie underneath it when we pass the toll booths. I think there are alerts out on you guys," Keith finished in a serious tone then took a big sip from his large coffee.

He popped in a device to the cassette player of the car and grabbed his iPod. "And now for your listening pleasure I give you the Scariest Band in the World, DeadBolt"

"I don't think I know them but the stranded can't complain" Janie said as a tinny methodical beat started emanating from the radio.

As they started digging into their food Janie realizing she did not have a knife started using a new nail file to cut and spread the cheese wedges on crackers. By the time the first song had ended the smell of the cheese odor overwhelmed the car.

"So who the Hell is Mrs. Valdez?" asked Janie, inquiring about the song.

"I don't care who Mrs. Valdez is," Bobby jumped in. "What the hell is that smell?"

Keith, anxious to fill both in on Mrs. Valdez, said, "Even Gary 3rd Degree Byrnes the writer doesn't know who she is, and the smell must be a skunk."

With an embarrased tone Janie quipped, "I'm sorry, it's my cheese."

"Is it bad?" Bobby asked.

"No, it's perfect, runny and pungent."

"Yeah, that sounds yummy," Keith came to Bobby's defense. "You realize that you are eating something that smells like garbage?"

"Smell is such a tease," Janie said as she offered a piece to the boys in the front of the car. "Think about it! All those great smelling foods BBQ, McD's French fries, Popcorn, as good as they taste, they can never live up to the smell they emit. It is just impossible for something to smell so good then taste even better.
But wheels of cheese, well the worse it smells, the better it tastes. I never have to worry about being let down."

"Well now that you put it that way, it makes me wonder," Keith said as he grabbed the cracker. Brought up to his nose and smelled it one more time he said, "As I figured smells just as bad up close," and tossed the cracker out the window.

Janie looked a little annoyed but started to make herself another cracker. Looking out the window she saw a sign "Welcome to New Jersey." It made her feel so warm inside. She missed her room, and she was so nervous what her mom and dad were going to say. Powering up her phone and checking it, she saw there were another ten texts. She started to text her dad. telling him, that they were getting closer to home and were completely safe. After the text she felt at ease, she also started to feel the length of the day and shifted around to get more comfortable in the car.

It didn't take her long to fall into a half dream like state, and as she was in the state of falling completely asleep the strangest thing happened. Keith quickly looked in the rear view mirror and then at Bobby, and in very authentic sounding Chinese said. "她是睡着了吗？"

107

Keith's sudden change of languages was enough to send Janie to dreamland. Bobby understood Keith's question perfectly but paused a minute to comprehend his sudden use of Chinese. He looked back at Janie who was out.

"是的" Bobby replied, letting Keith know that Janie was asleep.

Keith looked like he was about to say something, but Bobby beat him to speaking. He simply stated "Guam?" posed as a question of Keith's origin.

"Vietnam," Keith answered.

"That was my next guess."

"And how did you figure it out?" Keith expressed wonderment to Bobby's deduction.

"One, nobody beats Janie in a French test in Mrs. Kaya's class without speaking it, and two, your sudden yen for speaking Chinese."

"Nice Wu, I was born and lived there till I was almost 13. My dad is an engineer. He worked for a company that did a lot of work abroad. It seems like the company where he works was more French and American than Asian. However, the school I went to Chinese was the only language spoken, except for French, which you started taking classes in the first grade. By the time I got to Cali, I was quite the translator."

Keith paused for a moment and with a look of sudden awareness, "You know Wu, I never thought of it, but maybe I fell in with the skateboarders and surfers cause I spoke English so slow."

"You half pipe?" asked Bobby

"Whenever I can and the surf isn't breaking large," he said forgetting there wasn't much surfing in New York.

"I have a place for you. Well when I ever get to see daylight again. So why did you come from here from California?"

"Same reason I left Vietnam, my mom," Keith said, getting very serious. "She was sick very sick. I didn't know it at the time. I just kept blaming her for taking me away from my friends. Bobby, I didn't know nor would have I understood. What bothers me is that I never felt that I let her know I understood. I was so angry I am not sure if I ever let my mom know how much I really loved her; that none of the moving mattered. Bobby none of it mattered except getting as much time with her."

"I am sure she knew," Bobby said with sincerity and a better understanding of Keith. For some reason he thought of Keith's last name, and how even a Jackal needs his mom.

"Thanks, but I just wish I could make sure. It eats at me every day. This tooth eats at me every day," he said holding the shark tooth on his necklace. "She died right here. Bobby I never told Janie or Vanessa, they don't know. Please let me tell them. It didn't happen too long ago, right before I came to Bay Academy. Please don't tell them, believe it or not it makes things harder."

"Of course I won't say anything." Bobby assured Keith.

"She's buried in the cemetery across from Janie's house."
Keith kind of laughed at the small world it is.

"Are you serious?" Bobby turned and glanced at Janie.

"Yeah, why?" Keith's tone let Bobby know he was slightly put off being questioned.

Bobby, getting a little overwhelmed and beginning to think he might divulge Janie's secret, changed topics. "I'm sorry, No reason, I was just shocked, you know. So why did you want to know if Janie was asleep? You want to toss her cheese out the window?"

"No, Bobby I like her, but I get the feeling I am not the only one. I mean she followed you to Oswald's grave. Though it doesn't sound terribly romantic, I sense there is something more than just tombstones between you two. So do you have feelings for her?"

"Since I was 12," Bobby said like he has been waiting to tell someone for forever.

"That's a pretty long time. How does she feel about you?"

"Well, she thinks I am smart and funny."

"Look, I don't want to rush you or anything," Keith continued politely, "but maybe you could speed things up a little. I won't jump on your wave, but I won't sit in the ocean waiting forever either."

Bobby was a little taken back by Keith's confidence and aggression. He was beginning to give up hope of ever dating Janie, and this was most definitely moving this even closer to a reality. He also was getting kind of sick of the topic so using his debating skills he waited to Keith started to talk and overpowered him with his interjection. "I will work as fast as I can to clarify the situation."

He let Keith get off "Good" before he took over the conversation again and changed it to skateboarding tricks and surfing. Keith could feel himself trapped and would sound desperate if he went back to the prior conversation, so for almost the rest of the ride through Jersey the conversation was taken up by their best tricks and skateboarding injury stories.

As they were getting closer to GW Bridge, Janie started waking. It took a second for her to realize that she wasn't waking up in her own bed. It took only a second more for her to remember that she was about to get the worst punishment ever. It could have been the long trip, or the incomprehensible punishment to come; whatever the reason was Janie decided as she started waking that she was going to make a decision and a pick one of the boys in the car. This was going to be one of the most memorable nights in her life, so therefore it might as well have a little romance in it.

Bobby pointed to a sign for the GW Bridge as he mentioned to Keith that his dashboard gas light just came on.

Keith looked exasperated at the gas light which had just seconds ago illuminated. "I was hoping that we would make it back without having to fill up. But it doesn't look like were going to make it. Anyway, it will give everyone a chance to hit the head," he said.

Janie was very quiet and stated she had no desire or need to leave the car. Bobby on the other hand, had been bopping

111

up and down to the music and conversations for the last half hour trying to hide what his mother calls an overactive bladder. The ten minutes to the gas and rest stop seemed to take forever for him.

"I am going to park over here where it is a little darker," Keith said as he pointed to an area at the stop where there wasn't much light. There were a lot of cars parked there, as it seemed an easier place for a driver to get a quick nap. "I think it is best if we go one at a time," Keith said "So we don't draw any suspicion. Bobby was already in the process of bolting from the car as they all agreed.

"I guess Bobby had to go pretty bad," Keith said as he turned his body and face so he could to see Janie better. "Are you okay?"

"Yeah," Janie said as she stared into Keith's blue eyes. She started to drift just staring at those beautiful eyes. "It's been a long day, and probably going to be a longer next two to three months."

"Was it worth it? I mean whatever you guys were up to." Keith pushed the topic.

"No."

Keith looked a little surprised. He wasn't prepared for the one word answer. He didn't want to pry if Janie didn't want him to, and it definitely seemed she did not desire it. Keith was not sure what Janie desired. Janie wasn't quite sure either, but she was determined to find out what way her desire was leaning. And as she gazed deep into Keith's eyes she tried to feel that feeling she had the night she stared into the cemetery across the street. The feeling she had that night was like nothing she had ever felt. She remembered how she felt that she just needed to be next to Keith, to be holding him. Janie had never felt anything stronger in her life. But now as they sat alone in a car with her looking right in his sky blue eyes, the only thing she could see was Vanessa. Vanessa needed Keith and Janie was beginning to realize that she didn't.

Keith was looking right into Janie's eyes as well. With a confidence that he didn't quite understand, it had just seemed to build throughout the years for him. Yet his confidence could not overcome the blank feeling he was getting from Janie. He blinked to break the mood, and Janie immediately broke contact.

"So have you figured out what you are going to say when you get home?" Keith letting any chance of the moment totally fade away.

"No, I just hope I see my dad first."

"Dad's not as strict?"

"No, he just seems to understand me more," she said. "Does one of your parents understand you better than the other?"

"Kinda, but I don't want to trouble you with my problems right now. It wouldn't be fair."

Janie really didn't understand what he was talking about and she was beginning to loose interest in the whole conversation and she was relieved when Bobby rapped on the window for the door to unlock.

Keith hit the unlock button and motioned for Bobby to get into the back.

"We're about fifteen minutes from the GW Bridge, which means its nighty time for the two of you," Keith said as he pointed to the feet well, "And don't forget to tuck the blankies over your head."

At first, lying was very painful to Janie, but Bobby slid under her so that he was cushioning her from the hard floor and the bump in the middle. With each bump, Janie would squash Bobby; he would let out a little air like a dog's old abused squeaky toy. At first Janie thought he was joking, but after a while she realized it was because of the bump in the middle and she stopped laughing. Keith in the mean time had gone back to trying to convince them both that Deadbolt is indeed the greatest and scariest band. He even started to sing along with "You Don't Scare Me."

"Do you think he knows he should only sing in the shower?" Bobby let out between bumps.

"I think he sounds sexy," she replied, annoying Bobby.

"Whatever," Bobby said. "All I know is he's hitting those bumps on purpose."

Janie lack of sleep was causing her to blurt out quips with little thought and as they hit an unusual large bump, she jokingly let out, "Your little squeaks are sexy too!"

Bobby froze. He waited a second and tried to come up with an answer but froze again. Finally opting for comedy he yelled, "Keep hitting those bumps Keith."

"Sorry about that one," Keith said as he stopped singing. A second later after hitting another bump, he continued "And that one."

Bobby had become somewhat self conscious about his squeaks, but could not stop.

"Oh Bobby stop it, I'm losing control, stop it," coyed Janie.

They both giggled as Keith hit a huge bump that caused Janie to bounce a good foot into the air. When Janie landed their faces were much closer than before. Bobby let out a little air toot, and they both giggled once more. Janie looked at Bobby. The day had been one of those days that she will never forget.

The light had been getting brighter as there seemed to be more and more streetlights lining the expressway. Even with the added light, it was still fairly shadowy in the backseat. Bobby was quite taken by how the light that was striking Janie's face and hair.
Bobby's face was much harder to see as most of his face was shadowed by Janie's hair.

"I think I like this hairstyle most," Bobby joked.

Janie's frustration with her hair had been growing all day and this latest quip by Bobby had immediately sent her back into a foul mood. She was letting the anger build so that she could fully explode on Bobby.

Before she could achieve the proper level of agitation, Bobby followed with, "I really do like it the most. Maybe it's the lighting, but it looks," Bobby waited for the right word to come to him, "Enchanting."

Janie's anger continued to until without a doubt could sense that Bobby was not joking. He was lying there motionless; like he wasn't sure of what he said or that maybe what he said had just slipped out. Janie's anger had left but her intensity and adrenaline remained. She squirmed a little bit got her hands above her head. Pushing aside a half eaten bag of chips she grabbed Bobby head with both hands. One wrapped around the back of his neck and the other one kind of tugging his left ear. Bobby still motionless allowed Janie to pull his head toward hers until their lips hit. Bobby snapped out of his paralyzation and had he not been lying on his back might have jerked away. He pulled his head backwards for a second but he was not strong enough to overcome Janie's adrenaline fueled grip.

A few more seconds, and Bobby had stopped trying to resist. The bumpy circumstance was quite an obstacle for them to overcome as they both experienced their first true kisses. Soon they got accustomed to not smacking their teeth together. Occasionally, they would giggle a little when Keith would yell out, "Get close to each other and stay under the blanket."

Such complied commands and a constant voodoo like drone of Deadbolt's bass and guitars filled the car as it made its way through the ezpass toll and over the George Washington Bridge returning to New York in the heart of the Bronx. It didn't seem like a half hour more to Janie and Bobby as they switched between kissing, giggling, and touching each others' faces.

Bobby would still let out an occasional wheeze as they hit a bump. This would usually lead to another round of kissing. All their playing around made the half hour from the Bronx to Flushing seem like minutes. They didn't even notice as Keith pulled his car over a block away from both their houses. Lowering the radio Keith reached over to pull off the blanket and found Bobby and Janie side by side locked in another kiss.

Keith trying not to look surprised said, "I hate to inform you lovebirds, but it is time to face the fire."

Janie jumped up, and blushing and began to fix her hair. "Where are we?" she said, trying to hide her embarrassment.

"We are but a block away from both your fates, and I am guessing a block further than either of you will be aside from school for some time. And if you guys think I am getting any closer, well, you have a better chance of contacting Oswald," Not realizing that is exactly what they tried to do.

Keith looked around and shut the lights and engine, as Janie started to thank Keith for coming to the rescue. They all started to exit the car at the same time. The air was quite still, and all that could be heard were the crickets. The block was empty and only one house had a light on inside an upstairs window.

Bobby looked at his watch. "3:20," he said. "You made pretty good time"

"I would have better if my copilot had a stronger bladder."

Janie grabbed Bobby hands. They pecked one last kiss.

"You better get going," Bobby said as they broke apart. "Remember we went to a peace rally."

"I know good luck," she whispered.

Janie started to walk towards her house when Bobby ran to her and tapped her on the shoulder. "I forgot to tell you, you were wrong."

Janie again started to get annoyed. She wanted to walk in the fog of her first romantic moment before she had to face the reality of what lay in store inside her house. Now Bobby had just ruined that moment.

She swung her head around like a weapon and Bobby started to show a little nervousness as she said in more than a whisper, "I know Bobby, I know, I was wrong when I thought I was special. I was wrong to agree to take a bus to Washington. Was I wrong I decided to kiss you too?"

Bobby tried to look strong and tough. He was neither, but he stood up straight and looked the fireball in the eye and started to talk. "You were wrong when you said the taste of something that smells incredible can never live up to the expectations! I've been dreaming about what happened tonight for years. Yet those dreams never came close to being as amazing as it truly was. I can assure you I was not disappointed."

Janie froze again. Bobby sure had a way of turning her adrenaline into admiration. She stepped closer, reached out her arms, wrapped one around the back of his head and used the other to tug on his ear as she gave him one last kiss.

"Goodnight," Janie said as she stepped away from him.

Bobby let Janie have the last word and just put his hands to his lips to lightly blow a kiss as she started to turn and head home.

Bobby turned around and started to walk back to the car. Keith pretended to not be paying attention, but he had watched the entire moment; Not in a spying way but in a taking notes kinda way. Keith had learned in his early years of surfing that you could learn a lot by watching other people. He was man enough to realize, if put to the test, Bobby could muster what was needed to win the girl.

Janie started to run towards her house. Bobby watched her turn the corner and turned to Keith. He started to walk to Keith a little in a fog. Keith had seen that walk before many times at the beach. As Bobby walked in a fog in ways he couldn't remember what just happened but knew he would never forget it. Bobby stopped by the front of the car and felt the hood. "She's pretty hot" Bobby said as he took his hand away from the hood quickly.

"Not as hot as you two," Keith said with his patented grin. "You work fast Wu; and that line, you are a player. I guess I had you pegged wrong."

"Yes," Bobby said, still quite bewildered by the night and beginning to run out of things to say, "Well let that be a lesson to you."

"I am a player too," Keith paused for a second and then reached out his hand to shake as he continued, "And I play by the code. Besides there is this tall tender down that keeps coming by my desk that might be as crazy as your girl."

Bobby, as tired as he was, knew exactly who he was talking about and said, "Oh she's crazier, that's for sure."

"What is it about the crazy ones, Wu?"

"You never know what to predict," Bobby guessed.

"I will tell you one thing, its going to be one hell of a volleyball game." Keith flashed his grin as he stroked his chin.

"Oh I researched the positions. I am a setter," Bobby stated in a scientific matter.

"You know I would have thought after seeing you tonight that you were a striker," Keith said, again flashing a grin.

Bobby explained the reasoning behind his position simply with, "Balls have a tendency to hit me, not the other way around."

"Sounds like we will make a good team. Hey, shouldn't you be getting home? I got nowhere to go, I told my dad I was sleeping over at a friend's, but I figure every minute for you could be another week of grounding."

Bobby had forgotten for a half of second that he was about twenty hours late and in a heap of trouble. He immediately grabbed his bag and started to turn for home. Seeing the darkness of the cemetery, he suddenly turned back toward Keith.

"Look, in a couple of weeks when Janie's punishment subsides, tell her about your mom. Tell her everything. She might be able to help you. I really think she might," Bobby said to his teammate.

"OK," Keith promised he would do as they both quietly got back in Keith's car to head to Bobby's house.

A Break from Spring Break

Vanessa was in full campaign mode during the end of the break. She really was not sure what was happening, but she was raging a campaign to win Keith from Kristen, and now Janie. Janie had not returned her phone calls since the trip, as her phone and computer were officially confiscated and this made Vanessa even more nervous that Keith and Janie were now an item.

She thought about teaming up with Kristen to defeat this new adversary for Keith's attention, but she couldn't convince herself that any boy would be worth that. However, she still was mad at Janie, and could not control herself. Bypassing Kristen, she went straight to Amanda to talk about Janie and her attempt to run away. Vanessa was able to mention this because the Kelly's had called Vanessa's parents when they found out about Janie. Vanessa pleaded to know what the phone call was about and her mom finally gave her a brief breakdown of what she knew.

By the time school had started, Amanda had contacted the leader of almost every major clique, letting them know about how her mom got a call from Janie's mom. She told all the kids how Janie's mom said that the police were alerted that her daughter was believed to be a run away.

Janie showed up to school to whispers, snickers, and a whole new group of children making the face. Her Goth appearance was multiplied and exaggerated every day. Parents told their children that they didn't want their kids hanging out with Janie. Even Mr. Chambers, under the pressure of a few parents from the PTA, required new counseling sessions with the kids in senior and junior grades.

Janie's parents had punished her pretty severely even though with the help of the doctored pictures, she was able to convince her parents that they went to a peace rally.

Janie had talked to Keith and said it would be best for him if they didn't talk for a while to make sure he didn't get discovered for his role.

In that time, Keith and Vanessa had become something of an item, while Janie could not even contact her boyfriend. Occasionally, Janie would try to strike up a conversation with Vanessa; but Vanessa, not wanting to jinx her current status with Keith, would just brush the conversations off. For two whole weeks Janie studied alone, ate lunch alone, and rode the bus alone.

That was, until the Friday right after the French regents test. The test had gone okay for Janie, though she had been having a hard time studying of late. She especially missed Vanessa's impromptu quizzes of key words that she would then scribble onto her clothes or body. She had a knack for picking words that were on the test. As she swiped her bus pass into the fare reader, she remembered having forgotten to conjugate her verbs on one of the essays. Oh well, she thought, straight A's is a bit obnoxious anyway.

Janie scuffled into a two -seater and was trying to remember other parts about the test. She didn't notice the person next to her until he said, "CG, you got to help me."

"Excuse me," Janie said in a bit of a fog, and not realizing that it was Keith.

"Well, you don't have to help me, but Bobby told me to talk to you. He thought you might be able to help me," Keith finished his thought.

"And what does your girlfriend think? She is allowing you to talk to me?" Janie questioned while making sure to display her annoyance of the way Vanessa has been treating her.

"She doesn't control me. She also doesn't know, and it would probably be better if she didn't, though I think she misses you a lot. She always starts talking about you but she always makes sure to stop herself. I think she knows or at least feels like I was part of that night. Remember, I had to leave her house right before I made the trek," he reminded Janie.

"Let's forget that for now. What did Bobby think I could help you with, French?" Janie said sarcastically, still mad about Keith's perfect score.

"Vous n'en savez pas la moitié," Keith said with an emotion that Janie could never put into her French speaking.

"What?" she said not understanding his statement but fairly confident that he conjugated his verb.

"Janie, I speak French fluently, and I didn't learn it in LA. I also speak Chinese," he said in a way that was not meant to be snobbish or showy.

"What are you, some kind of super genius?"

"More like an alien," he responded.

"From Mars?" Janie said, not quite sure if she was joking or not at this point.

"No, Vietnam."

"What, are you a spy?" Janie said, again not sure if she was joking. "Wait, in the car as I fell asleep. I dreamt that you and Bobby started speaking Chinese."

"It wasn't a dream," Keith said as he let stared into Janie's eyes.

"Why Chinese?" Janie asked, quite confused at their need to speak Chinese.

"Well, we were talking about you," Keith said as the bus chugged its way past Francis Lewis Blvd toward Northern Blvd, which was the last big intersection before hitting Dominique's Market Supermarket.

"What about me?" Janie was getting a little put off by Keith's up-frontness.

Keith broke eye contact and looked down a little as he said, "I was asking his intentions."

"AND DID HE HAVE ANY INTENTIONS!!" Janie asked, in a more than slightly raised voice.

"It sure looked like he did," Keith answered, mimicking with his hands when he removed the blanket from the kissing duo in the backseat. "Besides that's all history now, the better man won, and there are some waves you are just not supposed to ride."

124

"So, you and Bobby, you just discuss this all like my feelings or intentions don't matter in this at all," Janie said loud enough for the entire bus to hear. She was beginning to really get angry, and she yanked the bus signal cord so hard that it sprung up and hit the roof when she released it.

"You don't jump on someone else's wave until you know they passed. Too many people get hurt," Keith stated, as if it was common knowledge.

"Will you stop classing me and all girls as some kind of waves!!?" Janie basically yelled as they both exited the bus, and for some reason stared at the sale signs in Dominique's window even though neither shopped for groceries. Chicken breast were always on sale for $2.39 and Janie had always wondered what they would be if they weren't on sale.

Taking a deep breath to be able to get enough of his thoughts out before Janie could find a reason to get angrier, he said, "It's an analogy, and maybe if you could remove yourself to see it, you would see that the wave is the strong thing here; Bobby and I, we are just floundering in the water but the wave is the strong one. It doesn't need Bobby or I at all. It knows where it's going. We need the wave; the wave is strong enough to get where it's going without either one of us."

Janie stopped for a second and blushed slightly. "Oh, man," she thought, boys lately had a way of turning her anger into something else. She theorized that this must have been somehow related to her becoming a woman. As they headed through the rear entrance of the cemetery, she started to feel desire to know more about the boy who just a few seconds ago made her blush. Again, like the night she was staring into the darkness, she just wanted to know more about Keith. Suddenly she remembered that you know never jump on someone else's wave. It was nice to think that some surfers might be girls, even if that meant there might be some male waves that had a sense of direction.

"Could you please just tell me what Bobby thought I might be able to help you with?" Janie asked as they walked on.

"You're about to find out," Keith said, as he pointed for her to turn down an aisle of tombstones.

Janie followed Keith about ten yards into the aisle when he turned to her and grabbed her hand. Janie thought about pulling her hand away until she felt the hand start to tremble.

She turned to look at the tombstone that bore the name Vivian Jackal.

"Is this…" but Janie's question was cut short as Keith answered.

"My mother," Keith said, not wanting to go through the possible list of relations that Janie might try to match the resident of the grave to.

Janie suddenly started to realize that the feeling she was getting might not be her becoming a woman, but more her becoming a medium. She concentrated on making Keith's hand stop shaking. They both said a prayer and Janie kind of tried to move Keith away from the grave. Being a possible channel was suddenly getting a little complex and she was hoping to have a private conversation.

"She got sick and we had to travel to find her the best help," Keith said after a while, as they had just about left the cemetery. "Every time we moved I would get upset with her, and blame her. Yet it wasn't her fault. Only, I could never understand that." Keith started to cry "I do now. Only it's too late. I should have told her I loved her more."

There was no doubt what Bobby was referring to. Outside the cemetery Janie was beginning to feel clearer in her mind. Clear enough to formulate that she might be able to help. They sat in Janie's backyard and Janie filled Keith in on the full background behind the ill fated trip. She told him if he wanted they could lie in wait to see Mrs. Mabbit to prove the things that happened.

Keith was quite easily convinced that Janie might be able to communicate, and told her there was no need to track down Mrs. Mabbit. Keith pointed out that little harm could come from a caricature as Janie had decided to call her sit-downs. He also told her that just talking about his mom with a friend helped him as well. After they both stopped sobbing for the second time, they made plans to make contact. Though Janie felt bad about it she decided that Bobby should not be there as he could possibly disrupt the communication. She would let him know once they could talk; it was not a secret, just something she had to do on her own.

Tomorrow afternoon they would meet in the cemetery. Keith had tried to do it earlier than 1pm but Janie convinced him that it really didn't work until after noon. Keith thought that maybe it was time zones and Janie agreed, figuring that it was as good as any reason to get to sleep till at least 10am.

127

Janie's punishment still had a week to go but starting tomorrow she was allowed to go on bike rides. Her dad was beginning to worry about her not getting out enough for air, especially on the weekends.

Sometimes You Had the Answer Hanging] Around Your Neck

Guitar lessons had been taken away from Janie for the month and it was the one punishment that seemed to not bother Janie. In fact it would have been a worse punishment if she had to go.

Janie woke up and even inside her room could feel that it was a cool crisp day. The humidity and signs of the coming summer seemed to be put on hold for this one day and Janie's hair, enjoying the change, decided to be somewhat manageable. It took her so little time to find an acceptable hairdo that Janie was actually dressed at 10:15. The last time Janie had dressed kind of Goth, but since she had started dating Bobby she had started dressing more colorful. As for dating someone, at least in her mind she was. Her punishment had left her with no communication devices at all. She had used the house phone to leave a couple of messages on his cell but kind of figured that he was in a similar situation. She was too scared to call the house because she did not want to foul up their peace rally excuse with info that did not agree with Bobby.

She assumed she was in a relationship, and the two weeks plus of acceptance time made the second date both more desirable and less intimidating; maybe because it would never happen.

These thoughts, and the day's coming events, ran through her head as she picked out quite a cheery outfit. It made sense; the last thing Keith would want to be reminded of was a funeral. She thought back to the time when she asked Bobby if she was a Goth child. He was right that Goths brings darkness to the world; Janie was bringing stuff out of the darkness.

Black was no longer her color. For a second, she thought about Mrs. Mabbit holding the drawing of her husband, then she thought about how much she herself missed Bobby. It wasn't the same but she understood to a small degree how hard it must be.

Janie might have gone a little overboard, and when her dad shielded his eyes from the bright color she went upstairs to tone it down a little.

She came down this time wearing a beautiful mauve top and skinny blue jeans. She hadn't worn the blue jeans since she bought them, always opting for her black pair.

She sat across from her dad at the kitchen table and poured some Special K into a bowl.

"Dad," she said as she poured milk. "You said I could go for a bike ride today."

"Yes I did, and yes you can, and tomorrow you get your phone and computer back." He paused and then added, "Oh and tomorrow we are going out to eat."

Janie was surprised by the going out to eat and inquired where.

"Cajun Pot. You liked it last time?" He paused for a sense of drama. "We are going with the Wu's."

Janie just sensed the whole second date becoming much more stressful, but she held her ground and tried not to look nervous, or give away her secret relationship.

"Dad, I'm glad it was you that answered the door," she said, after a pausing for a few seconds to figure how to get off the topic of the Wu's.

"What do you mean?"

"That night, I'm glad you were there; I was nervous it would be mom. You just seem to understand things better. You understand me better," she said as she smiled softly.

"Your mother tries hard Janie; sometimes you're not the easiest kid, you know."

"I know, I love mom, I'm just glad it was you."

"Well," he said in a whispery voice, "let's just forget it all, but I was very relieved when I saw you at the door instead of nobody at all."

Leaving the house, Janie grabbed her bike and headed in the opposite direction of the cemetery entrance as the plan was to meet on the north side of the cemetery, which was between Janie and Bobby's house. Janie was in no hurry and she noticed that since she lost TV and Internet, she was rarely late for anything.

She stopped her bike by at the corner of Laburnum] Lane and Pigeon Meadow Road, which wrapped halfway around the cemetery. Many of the streets had brick monoliths at their corners and that was where Janie waited for Keith, who finally arrived in his car with a Deadbolt song blasting from the open windows. Sticking out of the tied down trunk was his bike. He jumped out of the car and gave her a big hug. Keith went to the back of the car and unhooked the bungee cord latched to the trunk. Keith quickly inspected the trunk and its latch and asked Janie, "Why are there so many potholes in Queens?"

"They like it here," Janie chuckled. "Lots of tires for them to pop."

Janie had refused to get in the car with Keith as she was on a probationary bike ride and was not looking to be caught without her bike at her side.

They took off for the back entrance of the cemetery and Keith told Janie that he could not sleep last night. Aside from that update, they really didn't say much. It seemed that the moment did not call for words.

Janie started to talk as they entered the cemetery, in part to calm both their nerves. "The day of the bike trip, I didn't think much about it, but you knew your way through the cemetery. Well, the correct path is kinda tricky but you led us right through it, like you knew the way."

"Well, let's hope that your clairvoyance is quicker than your deduction skills," Keith said as he jumped off his bike. Lying on the ground, he looked at his tombstone and started to say a prayer. Janie got off her bike and started to pray as well.

After a minute and a few tears from both of them they settled down for the big task.

Janie took out her pad and pencil from her knapsack.

"So what am I supposed to do?" Keith asked.

"I'm not quite sure if sitting or anything helps, just concentrate on what you want to know. Whatever the question is just think about it." Janie was trying to Keith feel more comfortable, sensing his nervousness from his face and movement.

"Oh!" Janie smirked. "It helps if you take your shirt off."

"Really?" Keith said as he started to pull his sweatshirt over his head.

"I was joking," Janie smirked, as she hoped Mrs. Jackal had a sense of humor. You could tell as Keith fixed his shirt that Janie's joke put him more at ease.

"Just think of what you want to know, don't tell me or talk, just concentrate," Janie said in a much more instructional tone. "I will tell you when you can stop."

He stretched out on the grass leaning on Janie's knapsack and concentrated. After a couple of minutes, Janie began to draw. A few minutes later she signaled to Keith that he could stop concentrating and relax.

Keith concentrated for a little longer anyway, then he began to throw pebbles at an empty flower pot that must have been left behind by somebody who was planting flowers at a grave. He kept lobbing pebbles, attempting to land them in the pot. Every time he would toss one in the pot he would raise his hand and make crowd noises.

On the third successful try Janie, slightly annoyed, asked, "Why would crowds cheer you throwing pebbles into a pot?"

"I was pretending," Keith said, a little ashamed.

"Pretending what?" Janie tried to add to Keith's embarrassment.

"Pretending I was playing basketball," Keith said proudly, trying to brush off his immaturity.

"Well, shouldn't you use bigger rocks?" Janie asked, not letting him off the hook.

"It's a pretty small pot," he said meekly.

"Yes," said Janie looking at it, "and quite a big imagination."

"Are you done?" Keith said, referring to both Janie's drawing and her mocking.

"Yes, I am," Janie said, admiring the drawing. "I don't know what it all means or if it means anything, but I think it's you."

Keith took the drawing from Janie. He studied it for some time. "MOM," he said in an amazed voice. He stared at it for quite some time with a reminiscing stare that reminded Janie of the way Mrs. Mabbit looked the picture of her late husband.

"I was kinda expecting a WOW," Janie said, a little surprised to hear mom referring to a picture of a little boy.

"MOM is WOW upside down," Keith said to Janie. "I told you the word was special to me."

Janie visualized it for quite some time, getting madder and madder that she never realized that before.

"I know what it all means," Keith excitedly went on. "And yes, that's me. The woman you can't see is my mom, and the playground was in Vietnam. There was a location where the American company workers lived. They had a playground shipped in from the US. It was the coolest playground I ever saw. In that area of Vietnam you didn't see too many."

"You're sure that's it?" suggesting she look again with her hands.

"Janie, it's identical, like I am looking at the original plans of it. There is the club house and the slide; we used to make it into an obstacle course; it would always start and end with the slide. Nobody ever beat me, I was the champ." Keith said it like it was one of the proudest things of his childhood, then getting very serious he continued, "What is even more amazing is I remember the day."

"The day?" Janie asked, not being able to figure out what he meant by the day.

"Believe me, I remember it, in fact I have thought of it a number of times since my mom passed," he said as he picked up a bigger rock and showed it to Janie for approval. He lobbed it right into the pot, and Janie raised her hands and made a crowd cheering noise for Keith.

"I know why she had you draw it to," he continued as she noticed there were some tears in his eyes. "Janie, that day was the day when my mom told me we were leaving. She gave me the shark tooth, she used to call me, "鲨鱼," shark in Chinese. See, that is what is in the box that I am holding. She also told me that day that I could never hurt her; that she knew it was unfair to me; that she felt terrible. She just kept saying that I could never hurt her, that she loved me and she was so sorry for taking me away. I have thought about that day so many times, so many times I wondered if what she said was true. I wanted so bad to believe it was true, but now I know. She had you draw that so I would know it was true."

"It was this very shark tooth." He reached inside his shirt with a look of horror as he realized it was gone.

"I gave it to Vanessa!" he yelled.

"You what?" Janie was quite surprised and felt sorry for Keith realizing how hard it would be for him to get it back.

"I was thinking about my mom so much, and I wanted to get away from the thoughts. But I am so happy now. I am sure she is telling me she understands. She knows that I will always love her. She knows I am not mad at her."

First Keith, and then Janie started to cry. As Janie was crying she felt a release inside herself. She could feel the relief in Keith's mom, like she finally got to let him know. Janie sensed that somehow it must have been a very strong signal Janie was receiving. Janie was totally confident now that the times she was overcome with feelings for Keith as she looked into the cemetery that it was actually in part coming from signals from Mrs. Jackal or somebody. Janie studied the cemetery, the trees were really beginning to fill with spring life. Flowers for Easter seemed to be everywhere. Janie noticed another reliable trait of the cemetery, a small group of people in the location where she would always see people residing.

They both shot a few rocks at the pot and Janie got to three first, making crowd noises everytime every time she scored, while Keith pretended to make crowd jeering noises. They jumped back on their bikes and traveled back to Keith's car. Looking at the clock on the dashboard Janie realized she had only fifteen minutes and got ready to bike home.

"The Oswald thing makes a lot more sense to me now," Keith said.

"Yeah, but why didn't it work then?" Janie said, aloud in thought.

"Maybe it only works here?" Keith said, without much thought.

Janie paused and then it kind of hit her. Oh, Bobby would not be happy to not have figured out that it only worked in Calvary Cemetery. She hugged Keith and made him promise to tell no one, not even Vanessa.

Keith, fully understanding, did not protest and ironically assured her that he would take it to the grave if he had to.

Janie was home with minutes to spare. She plopped her bike in the garage, entered through the back door and headed for her bedroom. She made sure on the way up to see her dad so he could see she returned in time.

When she got upstairs, it was all there; computer, phone and TV. Technology was back, and Janie was quite relieved to have returned from her stone age punishment.

Her father had not attached the wiring of the computer as he figured Janie had a better understanding of where everything went. He was right, and though Janie was not as savvy as Bobby, she was able to get everything back up and running I no time. She booted up her PC and like a flash went to the most important thing on the web.

"Oh, my God," Janie spoke aloud in her room. "Lah, Lah, Lah is still in the top ten."

Janie jumped around to a couple of other sites before launching AIM. Just as Aim was coming up her dad popped his head through the doorway.

"So, I see you turned off my safety device. Well, I will have you know I turned it back on. By the way, I will know if you turn it off again. Janie, we give you a lot of responsibility. Your mother and I expect you to adhere to the few rules we do give you," he said in a voice showing his disappointment in her with turning off the spyware he had activated.

Janie watched as AIM popped up and Bobby's name popped as being online. She was about to jump off, as she wasn't prepared to talk to him. Today had been the first day that she really hadn't thought much about him, their trip and the backseat romance. Right before she could hit the close for AIM, a message came through from her Bobby.

B*[**Move asterisk in front of B][**:] Hi Janie, Long Time

"I know, I will be good I promise.[**,]" Janie replied to her dad as she started typing a response to Bobby.

**Janie:] Yes it has

*Bobby[**:] I missed you
**Janie: Yes it has
*Bobby: I missed you
**Janie Me 2

Janie instinctively typed as her dad left the room.

**Janie: Can you believe Blah Bla Blah is still there
*Bobby: Give it up/Hey did you hear about dinner
**Janie: Are they going to grill us
*Bobby: More than they do the steaks
**Janie: How have you been
*Bobby: Okay I just got computer back
**Janie Me2 and phone and tv
*Bobby: Mom made me give up 2 clubs and I pick up and babysit my brother those afternoons now
**Janie: That doesn't sound that bad
*Bobby: Its torture, its been torture not talking to you 2
**Janie: I have thought about you every day

Janie had gotten back into thinking of Bobby quickly, and felt right now if they were talking her last statement would have led to his stuttering of his reply.

*Bobby Me2…So are we???

Bobby thought of writing boyfriend girlfriend but was scared her dad might see later.

**Janie: We have to talk GTG. Going out with my dad.

It was not the answer Bobby was expecting, but Janie was trying to say as little as possible with the AIM recorder being on. Hopefully she would get to fill him in on the phone or somehow when they were at dinner.

Janie was glad to be off AIM with Bobby. She had really longed to talk with him, laugh with him, and to kiss him. It's just that the excitement of today was still pretty much dominating her thoughts. She very much wanted to tell him what happened, but with her dad probably reviewing every internet chat she was having, it wasn't safe to go into detail. She would try him later after her phone charged, but she wasn't sure if he had his phone back yet.

Dinner was meatloaf, though Janie always thought loaf was an inappropriate describer of her Mom's meat. It was more like dried mud with a hint of celery and onion. Janie would usually protest eating it, but today she suffered and ate all on her plate in attempt to stay on her good behavior. She was not looking to lose any of her freshly returned privileges.

After dinner Janie went upstairs to finish her homework; she tried Bobby on her cell but got his voicemail. Not sure if his messages were being monitored or reviewed, she hung up. She would see him tomorrow and hopefully be able to tell him what happened.

She finished up her math and thought about how much she missed her boyfriend and her best friend. Janie picked up her book report and read a couple of chapters of it. The loss of her technology until today did not help her get through her reading assignment and she still had half the book to read and the report to write by Thursday. Before she put the book down, she examined how many pages and figured she had 22 pages a night to read. It could be worse, she said to herself as she fell asleep.

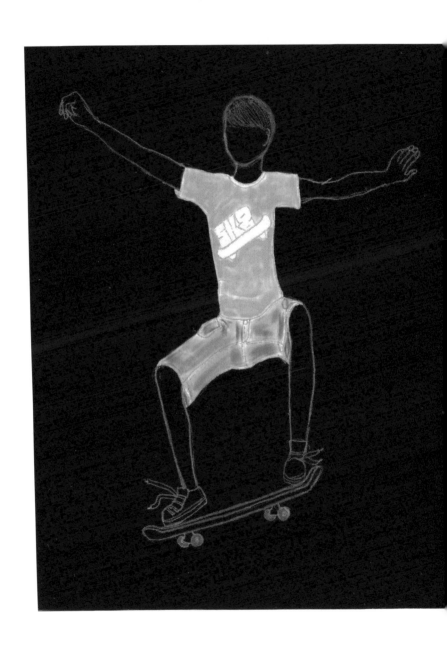

Sunday Night Fish Fry

The Cajun Pot was the Kellys' favorite restaurant and Janie's dad had suggested it when he had spoken with Mr. Wu.

Their talk was very cordial as they both were feeling the other out, trying to justify the blame each was leveling upon the other's child. As the families met in front of the restaurant, the mood stayed very formal except for Bobby and Janie. They hugged, making sure not to hug like boyfriend/girlfriend but more like best friends. It was a little difficult for Janie, and even more difficult for Bobby, who had been thinking about Janie nonstop since the trip.

Bobby took note that Janie had done her hair in a similar fashion to how she had it set when Bobby had made the comment that changed their Facebook statuses. Well, would have changed their Facebook statuses if they were not petrified of their parents snooping. In fact, Bobby had kept their relationship under almost total wraps telling only Nathan, his co-captain on the robotics team, who in turn refused to believe that Bobby had kissed a girl, let alone was now in a true relationship.

"Hey Girlfriend," Bobby said in a way that mimicked the constant TV saying that was popular on so many shows. Janie chuckled slightly and neither group of parents caught on to their inside joke.

The Wu's, Gordon and Hilary, were third generation, meaning both parents were born here. They would still talk in Chinese sometimes, but mainly to their parents. Gordon Wu and Tom Kelly both worked in New York City. Sometimes when Mr. Kelly took the 7 train they would see each other and wave. Mr. Wu was a senior analyst in the finance department of a magazine company. Currently, he was responsible for a women's hip fashion magazine called "Designs," and it always made him a little uncomfortable to talk about his work environment. Gordon's wife Michelle worked for an Asian market. She managed the relations with the vendors that had stores within the complex. Unlike Gordon, she mainly dealt with the Asian community and was a little more out of her element at the current time.

Tom Kelly was a manager in the phone company. He worked as a go between for the engineering department and the sales force, kind of like a highly technical customer relations type of person for larger based customers for his company. He would put all the pieces together; he wouldn't make the sales but he would work up much of the pricing. He wouldn't solve the engineering problems but would verify there was an actual problem that could not be fixed without engineering. He was a quintessential part of saving his company money and making the customer happy.

Right now, he was trying to make Mr. Wu and his family happy and feel welcome. The restaurant was very crowded and festive and with the motif of Mardi Gras around you, you did not feel like you were in a suburb of NYC.

Janie always loved the aroma of Cajun Pot. The spices and types of foods on the menu always made for a unique smell, which fit into her, "never can match an incredible smell with the subsequent meal," mantra. This, of course, had been squashed by Bobby's one liner and that special moment flashed in her mind. She snuck a peek at Bobby who, until he noticed her looking, had been studying the ambiance.

He grabbed her hand real quick and gave a squeeze as he winked at her. Bobby and Janie made sure to break hands before any parents noticed. The maître de approached and showed them to their table. The restaurant was quite crowded for a late Sunday afternoon, but even with the unusual crowd they were still able to be seated right away.

Janie convinced Bobby to order the alligator. When she saw an opening, Janie pulled Bobby out of his chair to show him the mural in the back of the restaurant. It was an ode to the carnival atmosphere of St. Paul Street during Mardi Gras Season. Though the mural was Janie's favorite piece of art, she had no real desire to show him it, she more wanted to get Bobby alone to tell him something else.

"I've missed you," Janie whispered. "I haven't stopped thinking about you."

Bobby was about to blurt out the same thing until Janie beat him to it. Now that she had broken the ice, Bobby got a little bit of a swagger about himself. A swagger that[**,] if he had spoken a second earlier, he would never [**have] had. "I missed you too," he simply said.

"I called your cell," she said "You get it back yet?"

"No, next week," he frowned.

Janie wanted to tell him something else. She wanted to tell him about Keith and figuring out how or where her powers work and her latest caricature, but she was afraid that Bobby would get too excited and would slip up at the dinner table.

"Janie, I think I figured out the problem." He kind of got into the topic she was avoiding.

Janie was pretty sure she knew what Bobby was talking about but asked anyway, "What problem?"

"Why you didn't make contact… you know," he whispered, afraid his mom's fantastic hearing would pick up too much.

Janie, knowing the answer, was about to say something. But Bobby didn't give her a chance. "It was your hair," Bobby continued, excited.

"What?" Janie said, confused.

"It was all the cherry blossom pollen," Bobby said, still very excited with his first scientific theory into the supernatural. "What do you have that is unique?"

"My hair?" Janie asked slowly, trying to make sure she was supposed to respond with that answer.

"Exactly, remember in DC you had all that interference," Bobby said with confidence to back his scientific theory.

Janie had tried to forget about the day her hair turned white, but now after this moment, it would never leave her. The memory and herself, filled with humor; she didn't want to laugh at Bobby, but he was really out of his element when it came to the supernatural. He could not pull himself from the traditional laws of science.

Janie started getting nervous that the parents might start trying to eavesdrop on them. So she motioned to Bobby and said, "Maybe, but let's worry about figuring it out when we get some time alone."

Bobby agreed, and they left the mural area and headed back to table. By the time they made it back to the table the appetizers had come; Cajun shrimp, stuffed eggplants, and chicken wontons. Mr. Wu commented on how good the wontons were, and suggested they try a BBQ and noodle house he loved next time.

Neither of the sets of the parents were terribly hard on them, and there was no reason to think that they had gone to DC for any other reason. The cause they went for was good, and thanks to Bobby's friend in the computer club they had the altered pictures to prove their participation. Bobby had even talked to him about altering some video, but it never needed to go that far.

One would have never expected Superman dialogue to be misquoted at the dinner, but all the adults agreed when Mr. Wu said to the two straight A students, "With Great Intelligence comes Great Responsibility, but you need to make sure you live up to the responsibility."

Dinner could have gone worse, and the families really got along very well for their first time out. Evelyn, Janie's mom, had been looking for employment back in her field in finance as she left her last company five months ago due to their moving to another location. Mr. Wu had told her there was an opening at the magazine. Evelyn said she would consider it but was trying to stay in Queens or close by in case something with Janie came up. She shot a quick "What could come up? Oh, maybe my daughter fled to Washington!" look her way.

Janie kept asking why Bobby never mentioned his dad worked in a fashion magazine.

"He's in the finance department," Bobby defended himself. "Besides, he has only been at that magazine for a couple of weeks. Before that he was working for 'PRIME.'"

"Prime," Mrs. Kelly said, looking up. "Isn't that the retirement magazine?"

"Was." Mr. Wu added, "It couldn't make it. Just couldn't get enough advertisers and the readership never took off."

"Bad circulation and no money coming in; I would always tell Gordon the magazine kept reminding me of my parents," Mrs. Wu said as she took a big sip from her wine glass adding fuel to the laughter.

"Well, I better get some front row fashion show passes!" Janie joked. "Or a least a magazine or two." She followed up with a more suitable request.

"I have some in the car," Mr. Wu said. "Magazines, not passes."

"You know what they say; artists can't be picky," Mr. Kelly chimed in.

"I thought it was beggars, dear," his wife said.

"Aren't they the same?" Tom laughed out quite glad someone threw him the line. He hugged Janie as the waiter brought the Dessert menu.

Vanessa Goes to War

Janie hugged her pillow as if it was Bobby. She was so happy that she got to spend some time with him, even if it wasn't alone time. She was even happier that the families got along as well as they did; perhaps Washington was a good thing. It forced Janie to do something that she had thought of from time to time since she was 12.

But now, late Sunday night after she finished her French homework, she thought a little bit about her Saturday's drawing session. She felt bad for Keith, knowing that it would be no easy task getting his tooth back from Vanessa, without starting an all out war. She did not realize that a war was already brewing.

Vanessa had gotten a call Sunday morning from Natalie. Natalie was a friend of both Vanessa and Janie and one of the few friends not associated with Bay Academy to have met Keith. Natalie did not think anything when she mentioned how she saw Keith riding bikes with Janie on Saturday. She was just letting Vanessa know how Janie must have been done with her punishment. Natalie had heard all about her running away from kids whose families knew the Kellys. Though the story the kids had told Natalie was quite elaborate, Vanessa never bothered to correct any of it. Angered by the news, she ended her conversation with Natalie stating Janie was lucky the incident didn't wind her up in jail.

Vanessa was still thinking of Janie as a possible adversary, and, with that, reached out to gather another ally in her fight. Vanessa had no idea of Bobby and Janie's magic moment that night, but always suspected that Bobby had feelings for Janie.

Bobby had just started surfing the web. He was actually trying to find out some information, about the Muellers, whose mausoleum he had visited. In the past couple of weeks, Bobby had become quite adept at researching cemeteries and their occupants. Apparently, Mr. Mueller was the heir of a tool making company whose symbol was a side view of a German Shepherd. Bobby laughed and couldn't wait to tell Janie.

Just as he was about to look up something else, his phone rang. Someone tried to contact him on AIM. Bobby was more than a little shocked to see it was Vanessa. She quickly let Bobby know of what Natalie saw. Bobby did not believe it but went to Chinese School with Natalie. He AIMed her and she confirmed that it was without a doubt the two of them.

Vanessa and Bobby hooked back up on AIM and made a plan to confront the two of them. Bobby was so upset that he went right along with Vanessa's plan. Tomorrow after school Bobby would wait by Dominique's. He was still being punished, but, he told Vanessa that it would work because he would just bail on robotics club. Robotics was one of the two clubs that he was still attending. If Bobby skipped it, they would have plenty of time to confront Keith and Janie. Vanessa would make sure that she had Keith drive them to Dominique's to pick up something after school. Bobby would make sure he ran into them. "And when the Q31 arrives the fireworks begin," Vanessa said in a very low tone.

Secrets Revealed

Janie had taken notice of the menacing stares that Vanessa was shooting her way Monday morning. She had hoped that things would start getting better this week with the big volleyball game tomorrow. Janie thought maybe Vanessa would start to simmer down; only this morning seemed worse than any since the trip. Janie was starving and jumped up from her seat when the bell rang ending fourth period history class. Mrs. Garret yelled to the class to make sure they remember their reports for Wednesday class, as they headed to the lunch room. Vanessa cut the line to make sure she was in front of Janie before they reached the counter in the lunch hall. Janie noticed that she had Keith's shark tooth prominently on display, as she was pushed aside by Vanessa. The counter was near the main entrance to the lunchroom, and the line for the hot food would often stretch out through the entrance and into the hallway. Janie was just about at the main entrance with Vanessa in front of her stomping her foot as if she was very agitated. Janie was salivating at the idea of any food in her stomach, as she tried to look past Vanessa to see what was on the menu.

The girls finally made it to the counter without a word being spoken by either. The counter area was filled with tacos, cheeseburgers, and some chicken dish that looked a little like her mom's chicken. Janie avoided the chicken and grabbed a taco off the rack. As she was reaching for an apple juice, Vanessa turned around and slammed her tray on top of her ex-friend's tray. Janie's taco went flying as the whole railing shook.

"You don't jump through somebody else's wave, or you get hurt." Vanessa shot a dagger like stare at Janie before she picked back up her tray and went to sit down with Amanda and Kristen.

Janie wasn't quite sure what to make of Vanessa's threat. She was sure Vanessa was mistakenly quoting Keith with the first part. However, with the way she slammed the tray and the look she gave, Janie was confident that she meant the "you get hurt" part exactly as she stated it. All that aside, Janie really never connected the threat with the possibility that Vanessa had heard about and was now misinterpreting her and Keith's meeting. Janie sat down by herself as far from the Prim and Proper as she could. She looked over that way at one point to see Vanessa showing Kristen the best technique to make the zombie like eyes of "the face."

Janie felt the tension for the rest of the whole day and not just from the Vanessa, but the other Prim and Proper as well. Kristen tried to do the face at one point when Janie raised her hand to answer a question in geometry, but it came out as more of a constipated old lady face. Janie had barely seen Keith, though at one point in the morning when they were in the hall he had said to her, "I have something to show you." However, Keith was quickly dragged away by Tom who apparently was on Keith's containment patrol. They never got another chance to meet, and Janie had wondered what he was talking about.

When the day ended Janie was quite glad to see the usual portly bus driver of the Q31 pull up across the street from the school.

Janie pulled out a pad and started to draw; lately drawing had taken on a new meaning to her and she had almost forgotten how much the non-channeling type of drawing relaxed her. She started to lay down on the paper a very elaborate wedding dress and veil. She had just finished as the bus approached Northern Boulevard. Janie tucked her small drawing pad back into her back pack and pulled the cord for the next stop. Vanessa's plan had worked perfectly, and, as the bus doors opened in front of Dominique's, there stood the three of them having just met.

Vanessa noticed Janie getting off the bus first and said, "Oh, look who it is." Vanessa tried to look surprised, but she still looked more agitated than anything. She was wearing a red shirt, and right now her face seemed to mimic its color. Janie did not feel comfortable about the sudden meeting, as not only did Vanessa know nothing, but there was still much she had to explain to Bobby. She wanted to look for Keith for support but figured that would be the worse thing she could do.

Vanessa walked up to Janie, holding Keith's hand, and with no sincerity she said, "Janie sweetie, how are you? So what did you do this weekend?"

Janie now realized that someone must have reported Saturday to Vanessa, and that she was totally blowing it out of proportion. Janie couldn't really set it straight without explaining everything to both of them so she decided to play it quiet. "Sunday, we went out to eat with the Wu's," Janie stated, not ready yet to divulge where she was on Saturday. Bobby offered no help to Janie, as he slowly glided his bike closer, occasionally touching the ground with one foot or another to add a little bit of speed.

"What about Saturday, dearie?" Vanessa pressed on.

"Nothing special," Janie said, hoping Keith would interrupt. Only, Keith could not say anything either, as Janie had asked for his silence.

"That's not what my spies tell me," Vanessa yelled. "They saw you having a wonderful bike ride with Keith. My darling Keith," she said as she looked over at Keith with a menacing stare similar to what she had been dishing out to Janie all day.

"It's not what you think," Keith said, finally realizing why Vanessa was so upset.

"Oh, and I suppose that note you have been carrying around in your pocket for the last two days and the way you asked for your necklace isn't what I think either," Vanessa yelled.

Keith instinctively touched his pocket to make sure the drawing was there. Vanessa was correct that he had been carrying around something from Janie, but it wasn't a note. He looked at Janie and asked her a not so simple request, "Please," hoping she would let him show them the drawing.

Janie thought about it. She looked at Vanessa and said. "Vanessa, you're my best friend." She continued to stare at Vanessa's face. It showed signs that she wanted to return the best friend testimonial. And though Janie wasn't sure if it was the right decision she decided to fulfill Keith's request. "Take out the picture," Janie said to Keith.

Keith took out the illustration of his youth. Janie noticed that it looked like it had been handled quite a bit since Saturday when she drew it. She then quickly glanced at Keith's face to make sure he was okay with what was happening. Janie could tell, Keith seemed to be relieved, as he handed the drawing to Janie.

"This is what we did Saturday," Janie stated, as she walked closer to Vanessa to show her the drawing.

"You guys drew a picture? It's not very good," Vanessa said, looking to insult anything she could. As Vanessa grabbed the drawing out of her hand, Janie quickly released it not wanting the drawing to be ripped. Vanessa continued to look at it with disdain.

"It's amazing," Keith said grabbing it back, afraid of what Vanessa might do to it. "We didn't draw it together, Janie drew it for me."

Janie doing anything for Keith was enough to overflow Vanessa's anger into action, and she grabbed at Janie. Keith quickly dropped the drawing and grabbed Vanessa, holding her back as he blurted out, "Besides, it was Bobby's idea."

Hearing the idea was Bobby's, Vanessa switched directions trying to go after Bobby.

"Your idea!" Vanessa screamed as she barreled toward Bobby. "What were you thinking?" she yelled in his face.

"I wasn't, I mean, I didn't." He turned to Keith mad and said, "I didn't suggest you guys go bike riding together, and draw a picture of a playground. I thought she might be able to help you with your mom," Bobby finished while studying the picture he had picked up and seeing nothing that would lead him to think that drawing was about Keith's mom or the anguish that he was going through.

Vanessa settled down slightly as she started to realize that more than a romantic bike ride might have taken place Saturday. With glimmers of hope that no romance took place at all that day, she tried to compose herself a little and waited for a full explanation.

"It did, Bobby," Keith said excitedly as he fixed his shirt, which had gotten all out of whack when he was holding Vanessa. "It set me free from all those years of worrying. All those years of wondering; could she see that I really didn't hate her, and that I really didn't blame her."

Bobby continued to look at the drawing. "How? I don't see anything but a kid and dog at a playground."

"Not just any playground. It's the old playground in Vietnam, in the complex where I lived," Keith said with pride. "The boy is me, the dog is just lucky."

"Dogs do not stand for luck," rallied Bobby.

"No, that is the community dog Lucky," Keith said, annoyed to be defending the drawing. "You know, Bobby, some things are not covered in your Asian studies, and I assure you that stray dog was very lucky to be adopted by the community of foreign workers."

Keith dug into his other pocket and pulled out a picture. "You see this kid at this playground?"

Bobby took the picture from Keith and compared it to the drawn playground. The angles of the drawing and the picture were slightly different and the boy he was referring to was hanging from one of the monkey bars, but it was obvious that the two parks were almost identical. Bobby continued to study it as both Janie and Vanessa started to look over his shoulder.

"You mean, you made contact?" Bobby asked, a little upset that he was not part of it, but even more upset to find out this way.

"Yes, I wanted to tell you so bad yesterday, but I was afraid that our parents would overhear," Janie went on, relieved that Bobby finally knew. "Plus I can't write a thing about it on my computer right now, my dad has every security setting maxed."

The only thing Vanessa knew at this point was that Janie had drawn a playground from a picture, and as she had pointed out it wasn't even that great a picture. Seeing Bobby and Janie conversing together, Vanessa turned toward Keith for an explanation.

At Keith's suggestion, the four started to walk in the direction of the cemetery. Keith explained as much as he could to Vanessa while Janie told Bobby about the caricature and what it meant to Keith. She didn't get into the whole theory of her powers only working in Calvary Cemetery. As they neared the back entrance of the cemetery, Bobby and Janie found a reason to stop talking. Bobby had been holding hands with Janie as he walked his bike with the other and when they stopped walking he laid the bike down. Bobby pulled Janie a little closer and they hugged. As they embraced, Janie said softly, "I'm sorry."

"What for, you didn't do anything wrong." Bobby kissed her on her cheek. "See, I told you, that you were special."

He grabbed her by the back of her head, and with his left hand reached into her mane of hair. Finding her ear, he tugged on it in similar fashion to Janie first kiss technique.

Vanessa had just about been brought up to speed about Keith, his mom and life in Vietnam. Overwhelmed by the whole experience Vanessa turned around to talk quickly to Janie, and she was brought up even faster on Janie's relationship with Bobby as she saw them locked in a kiss.

"Are you out of your mind?" Vanessa said in way that seemed rehearsed, as if one day she knew she was going to say it.

Bobby's head shot up and he responded, "Yes, I believe I am."

Vanessa pushed Bobby out of the way, saying to him, "I was talking to her, I was already fully aware that you were out of your mind!" She turned to Janie and with true joy in her eyes said in earnest, "I am so happy for you. You two are perfect. You really are." She glanced at Bobby with a smile to show she was only joking with the out of the mind comment.

Janie could see the relief in Vanessa's eyes. The fact that Bobby and Janie were together and Keith witnessing it was heaven to her. Vanessa no longer had to hate Janie. She could simply be her best friend again, and Janie could see it immediately in her face.

Keith, looking back at the whole escalation, simply came out with, "My girlfriend has spies. Cool."

Bobby released Janie completely and turned to Keith saying, "I wouldn't get too excited; I heard she has assassins as well."

"So I guess it all has to do with that spot you always ask me about," Vanessa said nonchalantly.

"What are you talking about?" Bobby asked, annoyed by Vanessa adding to the confusion, but Janie just sat there shocked. She had never connected it but now that Vanessa threw it out there it made sense. It must have something to do with that area.

Janie looked at Bobby and explained, "I didn't tell you yet, but Keith figured it out. It only works in this cemetery."

Bobby looked very annoyed now. "What about the hair? I mean, it could have been the hair and the interference from the pollen."

Keith and Janie joined Vanessa in a baffled look at Bobby. "I mean it only worked here," Janie said to Bobby, hoping to end his denial.

"Yes, but we only tried it here and the only other time you were covered with pollen. I really feel that it was the interference." Bobby started to lay out his scientific theory.

He turned to the group as a whole and explained his theory, "I fully believe that Janie's hair acts as an antenna of sorts in her communication."

"Her hair?" Vanessa said in almost the exact tone that Janie had when Bobby suggested his theory to her at the Cajun Pot.

"Exactly!" Bobby said, once again not picking up on the baffled question-like response from Vanessa.

Before Bobby could get out any more of his theory Janie interrupted with something she had not told anybody. "But what about the feelings?"

"What feelings?" the rest of the group asked in unison.

"The feelings I had about Keith," she said, causing Keith to blush. Vanessa's face was slightly redder and again getting close to her shirt color, but she was not blushing. She also wasn't very patient in waiting for further explanation.

"What feelings dearie?" Vanessa said. Not allowing an answer she went on, "Keith, sweetheart, did you know about these feelings?"

Keith shrugged his shoulder, slightly worried that Vanessa was about to signal her assassins, spies or commandoes allegedly at her disposal.

"Nobody knew about the feelings," Janie announced.

"Yes, till now. Now we all know NOW!" Vanessa turned to Bobby. "Do you have any feelings that you would like to announce to the world?"

"Well I am a little upset and scared," he responded.

"Can I explain?" Janie pleaded, while grabbing Vanessa's arm to get her attention.

"Yes, please do," Bobby chimed in, letting Janie know that not just Vanessa was getting a little irritated.

"See, the day of the bike trip, it happened right as I was riding through the cemetery. I can't explain it, but it was like right when Keith spoke I just wanted to know everything about what he had to say. Then again that night when I was looking out into the cemetery, I had that same feeling again." Janie did not bring up the kissing image as it wasn't going to do anything but make Vanessa and Bobby madder

"Was this after or before we AIMed]?" Bobby continued to be a little confrontational with his questioning.

"After, as if that matters," she continued. "Listen! So the last time I had the feelings was Friday when Keith came and told me about how unhappy he was about his mom, but they didn't start till we got close to the cemetery."

"So those feelings are gone? You know all Veritas vos **liberabit**," Vanessa said, emphasizing the Latin for free.'

"Yes, all gone, but thinking now those feelings, they must be part of what causes me to draw, and it only seems to happen here."

"But the Keith ones are gone, Vooossh gone?" Vanessa asked one more time for confirmation as she waved her hand in an attempt to emphasize the feelings having left Janie.

"Yes, gone with the wind. Can we move on? So, I never had these feelings anywhere else, and I think I had similar feelings when I saw Mrs. Mabbit looking at her drawing. Like I was a loved one reaching out to her, trying to touch her. Bobby what do you think? I think it all has something to do with Calvary Cemetery." Janie looked at Bobby hoping he would agree.

Bobby picked his bike back up and mounted it. "I'm sorry," he apologized "but I need to sit when I theorize." He pushed back and went through all the times. He picked up one foot at a time, rocking his bike as he sat on the seat. He still wasn't sold on the concept. To him, it just didn't make total sense. Keith and Mrs. Mabbit had this connection with their caricatures, but the two times he queried the dead these feelings would not be channeled through a loved one. They were simply answering the question posed with no great loved one or kin connection. He still felt it was not isolated to Calvary Cemetery.

Suddenly, Bobby got slightly sidetracked in his logic. If he was to debate the side that these feelings were not associated with the ending result, and it was not isolated to Calvary] Cemetery], to some degree he would be arguing that Janie's desire about Keith was her own and not caused by his mother's desire to know more about her son. He swayed his bike one more time, looked up with his head, blinked, and said, "Keith, you were right, very intuitive of you."

160

Keith clasped his hands together as he nodded an acknowledgement to Bobby. "If you were there, you would have guessed the same." Keith gave credit to Bobby's deductive ability.

"Well, what about my theory, that it all has to do with that area?" Vanessa asked, with an excited voice. Her anger had completely subsided, and she seemed to be ready to contribute as part of the supernatural exploring team.

"I still don't even know what you are talking about nor do I think I want to," Bobby said.

But Janie just stood there frozen for a moment; having to defend the (outside her own body) feelings, she had forgotten about Vanessa's theory. "I know this sounds crazy, but I think she is right," Janie said to Bobby. "I had never really thought about it but I think that we need to do one more drawing. Only for the life of me I have no idea what we should be asking. We need to go to that area I had mentioned to you where the weird people always are."

Janie turned to Vanessa and thanked her for the suggestions. Vanessa grabbed Janie's shoulders and pulled her into her, giving a big hug. Their size difference was quite noticeable and one of the main reasons that Vanessa was vital to the volleyball team. Which Janie brought up with the question, "So we are teammates again?"

"We were always teammates; once a Rebel always a Rebel," Vanessa said referring to the Bay Academy volleyball team. "More importantly, we are partners again, and I think our adversaries and boyfriends would be much advised to come tomorrow and see what they have signed up to face."

161

"Oh, that's right, I forgot to tell you," Janie said, turning to face Bobby. "Tomorrow is the big volleyball game against Alvarez High. Can you make it? Cause I got a feeling that the girls from Luis Alvarez are going to find they messed with the wrong isotope." Bobby laughed at Janie's predication while Vanessa asked Keith what an isotope is.

Janie looked at Bobby with puppy dog eyes, hoping he would make the game. Keith helped the cause, saying, "I can pick you up in front of your school." Keith's offering in part may have been an attempt of not having to explain isotopes and radioactivity to Vanessa as he continued. "I think it's best we scope out the competition, especially when they are in cute volleyball uniforms."

"There is nothing cute about our volleyball uniforms, especially with me taped up like a mummy," Vanessa said, forgetting about her other question.

"OOHH, Cemetery Girl and the Mummy, sounds like the traveling team from Transylvania." Keith laughed, as he stuck his arms out and pretended to move like a mummy.

Vanessa quickly flashed her anger as she said, "Nobody heard, said, or saw that! Am I making myself clear? "

They all quickly agreed to never say the word mummy again, as Vanessa jokingly signaled off her assassins.

Somebody Spiked the Water

Coach Hill walked to the head of the bus. She had been pretty quiet the whole bus ride. It wasn't a far ride, but for Coach Hill quiet was not the norm. Occasionally, one of the girls would turn around and shoot a number one sign for the Rebels, or mouth that they were going to kick some ass. Ms. Hill would go along, but she was not her usual self.

As she looked out over the girls, she got a little teary. She blew her whistle once, instead of repeated times, like she usually would to get their attention. The change of procedure was immediately noticed by the girls and they settled down quicker than usual. Janie and Vanessa were towards the back of the bus. Vanessa, since she was little, always opted for the back of any bus as she felt more comfortable about her height in the back.

Rhonda, one of the seniors, broke the quiet and yelled, "Come on Ms. H., let us have it!"

The coach shushed her with a nod and looked to the ceiling of the bus. "I wasn't sure if I should let you guys know, but this might be our last game." Most of the girls had not caught on to the seriousness of the coach's speech, as they thought she was referring to the seniors.

"There have been a lot of cuts at the school, and I want you guys to know there is a good chance that we are on the block for next year," Coach Hill said, making sure the girls started to understand. "I wasn't sure if I would tell you this, but I think it's fair for you to know; if we win this game there is a much better chance, in fact, a really good one, we will be back next year. I know it is an unfair pressure to put on you, but it's more unfair to not let you know what you are playing for."

Kristen began to grow very irate. She was second in line to Bridget for captain. Just like her status as a Prim, Kristen was always second in line, and had plans to change that in a big way with the team next year.

The only thing that upset Kristen more than being second in line was her height. Her whole life Kristen hated how she towered over almost everyone, and the only joy she had gotten from it was volleyball. Though Vanessa had her in height by a couple of inches, nobody could touch Kristen on the court. She could have been captain or co-captain, but she felt it was too early; when Kristen finally became captain, it was going to result in a championship. She wanted to be the one to lead the Rebels to the Regionals, and she felt this year they were one game away. This was the game she felt they couldn't win, but now all that had changed. She and her teammates had ten minutes to change that fate.

Kristen headed up to the front of the bus and joined the captain. As Ms. Hill was beginning to lose the battle she was having with her tears, she gathered her emotions and continued, "I can't tell you what you girls mean to me, what this team means to me, and I won't go without fight! Don't you guys go without one either."

The bus driver looked at Ms. Hill trying to ask if he should open the door. she signaled not yet and asked the group if anybody had something to say.

Bridget stood up. "I think we all know who contributed the most to us getting here. She passed up the chance to be captain to allow me to have the chance. She worked harder, worked us harder, than anyone here. And I say she deserves the chance to play next year. You all deserve the chance."

Kristen stood up. Bridget didn't need to announce her. "I don't want to be on the team that loses the last game played by the Rebels. I don't think you do either!" Kristen yelled. "And if it happens, well then they're going to have to hit that ball right through me!! Now let's go out there and show them what B-A-D ASSES the B-A Rebels can be."

She turned and pounded on the door and Harry obliged releasing the handle.

Kristen bounded down the few steps while in a war chant; the other girls stomping and shaking the bus as they exited. Coach Hill exited the now visibly shaking bus with the girls stomping and pounding the outside of it. Harry couldn't car; he had been touting the Rebels around for the last 12 years and was glad to see they weren't going down without a fight. And as the bus swayed, he started honking the horn to the stomps.

The noise and antics caught the eye of some of the opposing team and their families as they entered the school. Ms. Hill was happy to see the concerned look on the opposition's faces. And as the team started to enter, they sang out their modified Billy Idol chant: "With a Rebel Yell we'll cry Score Score Score." Rhonda thought up the chant two years ago but was afraid to tell anyone. Feeling this was the inevitable end of the Rebels she had started it. Some of the parents knew the song and, after hearing the words a couple of times, sung along with their kids.

On the sidelines Coach Hill blew the whistle once, and the team, reminded of the importance of their antics, they quickly quieted down so the coach could call out the lineup. The starting front line, being Bridget, Kristen, and Vanessa from left to right, were announced without surprise. Maggie, the defensive specialist, was wearing the blue libero jersey, and started in the middle. The rest of the girls were in their off white uniforms. Since there were only seven members on the team and the best six were on the court, Ms. Hill wouldn't be] doing much subbing except to keep Maggie staying in the backfield.

Janie looked over at Vanessa as Ms. Hill yelled out last minute instructions. Janie was still trying to get a true feeling of the frenzied state the girls had displayed.

She looked over at Vanessa expecting her to be confused as well, but instead saw intensity in her eyes. Vanessa just kept staring at the girls from Alvarez High. Since she started dating Keith, Vanessa had been happy for the first time, truly happy. Now that she had made up with Janie her life seemed perfect. Volleyball somehow fit into that and nothing nor any opposing team was going to stop her from being happy.

Janie, on the other hand, though a participant in the chanting, could live without volleyball. She enjoyed it somewhat, though at times the ball really hurt. The only reason she was on the team was that Vanessa begged her to join last year when the team lost a few seniors and was almost getting to small to be a squad. It was ironic as they took the court she was the Rebel to hit the first serve. She wasn't the best server, but she was the weakest of the six at the net, and this kept her from it as long as possible.

Ms. Hill called the defense she wanted and signaled Janie to serve deep to the left side. The first serve was not a good sign for the Rebels as Janie's serve was easily picked up by a backfield and passed to the left front who set for the center. Vanessa was so intensely watching the other team that she didn't even jump for a block. She marveled at how the LA's center waited for the last second to spring down so fast that it almost gave her extra momentum on her up-jump. She smashed it mid field, and as the ball hit the court a lot of the hysteria the Rebels had built up went with it.

The first game went fairly easily to Alvarez High 25 to 21, but Ms. Hill hadn't lost faith; it was the best score they had ever put up against the Reactors and it was best of three. She could see a look of concern in their coach's eye as she watched her team pushed harder than usual for a win.

Ms. Hill settled on the same set up for game two, but had noticed Vanessa playing harder than usual and almost flipped her with Bridget to give her more front action. Janie had noticed Vanessa's efforts as well. She could see her putting in 120% and decided if it was that important to her friend then she should put in 130%. She wasn't saying to

167

herself she should try harder than Vanessa, she was more estimating that her 100% was really a 92% effort from Vanessa. By the time she had finished the calculations Ms. Hill was handing her the ball to serve. She took it from her and said, "I want to hit it to the right."

Hitting right was more dangerous, as it put much more out of bounds into the landing spot, but it would more likely start the block on Vanessa's side.

"What if I told you to hit to the left?"

"It would probably be a miss-hit to the right side," Janie said, not prepared to change direction.

"Well, then nail it," she said as she handed the ball to Janie.

Bridget and Kristen did a double take when they saw where Janie was going to put the serve. They didn't protest though, they knew Vanessa was sharp today and LA's right side was weakest.

Everybody could see the change in Vanessa but herself. Vanessa was not really in control of her changes when she got mad. However, those changes were quite noticeable to others. She would think faster, move faster, react faster, all the time with no change to her body. No increased adrenaline, no raise in her heart rate, just an intense red in her face like warrior paint. It was almost like her body would morph to a higher level of ability, with all the adrenaline still accessible to raise it even higher.

Janie served a nice shot down the line. LA set a return from the right, and Vanessa was the only chance to block. She got real high and in perfect position laid down the block that gave the opposing front no chance to return.

Janie put three points up before she was done serving. After LA gained a point from their service, Vanessa added another two for Bay Academy on aces. Kristen looked at Bridget after the second and asked, "Who spiked her water with HGH?"

"I don't know, but I am drinking from her bottle in between games."

BA easily won the second game 25 to 14. Ms. Hill was sure that the Alvarez High team played soft once they saw the game was too far gone, not wanting to give anything away for the third game.

The Rebels celebrated their second game destruction with their chant again, as the referee warned them to keep it down.

The third game was thirty seconds from starting and Ms. Hill pulled the team together. "Look, they laid up the second half of the game. Don't get upset if they score a couple of points early, just stay focused and don't give up on any points. It's not that long a way to fifteen; remember we only go to fifteen." The buzzer sounded and they headed onto the court.

"I think we know the lineup by now," Coach Hill said, as she blew her whistle. She had thought about putting Vanessa on the left to give her more time at the front, but did not want to mess with the way the team was playing.

She handed the ball to Janie and asked her, "Right?"

"Well, since you say so," Janie said.

At the line Janie bounced the ball three times and served out of bounds. It was not the start they wanted. And it didn't get much better with Vanessa serving either. But the girls fought back quickly and the match was very close throughout.

The coach was right; it was not a long way to fifteen with both teams getting there quite quickly, it seemed to the players.

And ironically, with the score tied at fifteen it was again Janie's time to serve. It was also what Ms. Hill viewed as her Rebels' last chance. With Vanessa moving off the front line, the coach knew it was now or never for her team. She thought about taking her last timeout, but then figured all she would do is add pressure.

Janie bounced the ball three times and served down the right line. The Alvarez backcourt called out "NO" and let it hit the floor. Only by a miracle some part of the ball caught the line. Rebels went up16 to 15 on the easiest ace of the game, as the Alvarez backcourt was sure it was heading out.

Janie was ready to serve again when Ms. Hill sent signals for Janie to serve left. She had served every point of this game to the right, and she thought it might catch them off guard. The serve was nothing special and the back girl bumped up front getting ready for a smash up the center. As the ball rose Vanessa saw the fake being set up. Kristen and Bridget didn't, and they were both readying a block to the left center. The opposition rose and so did Kristen and Bridget; only the Alvarez team wasn't about to spike. It was a decoy for a simple tap to Bridget's side. The backcourt had bought into the fake and they were moving to the middle. Only Vanessa saw it was a decoy and she broke from her position, racing for the area where the ball would fall. As she broke she wanted to get Janie's attention, knowing most likely the others were moving the wrong way.

"Veritas," she yelled as she flew across the court. Janie, hearing the cry, took off. She had good momentum by the time Vanessa dove saving the ball from the ground and hitting it quite high. Though the ball was still rising it was headed in the direction of their backcourt and as well was well out of bounds. That didn't matter to Janie. The left guard had also had been moved out of position by the fake and there was only one person who had a chance at the ball. And as Janie dove for it she returned Vanessa's cry with "VOS!"

Janie got even more height on her bump than usual and managed to direct it towards the net. Vanessa had not paused after her first hit, she had slid a good five feet over the out of bounds. Vanessa finished sliding to almost where the stands started, but she had immediately popped up to her feet. She instinctively started running to back to the court and was about half way there when she heard Janie's cry out of VOS."

As Vanessa dashed she saw Bridget and Kristen were still tangled on the floor from when they tried to redirect their jumps for the block. Vanessa knew the only other person aside from herself in position to attack the ball was Rhonda, but she was the Libero and was only allowed to bump the ball, not attack it over the net. She was also fairly confident that she would not finish the Latin phrase even if she was the Libero. Vanessa was running close to parallel to the net and just about close enough to jump for the spike. Only the way she was facing was going to force her to toward the opposition's sideline, and as she took to the air she realized there was only one place to aim. It was almost like Vanessa bounced off a trampoline, and Coach Hill was sure she was a foot higher than Vanessa's normal jumping height. She was just sailing directly above Kristen and Bridget, and when they saw Vanessa coming flopped back on the ground as low as they could.

The snap thud of the contact actually echoed as did Vanessa's cry of "LIBERABIT[." Vanessa watched as the ball went exactly where she aimed it, into the face of the left back fielder for Alvarez High. The impact caused the sweat to bounce off the girl's face, right before she and the ball hit the ground in a unison thud of defeat.

Seeing the girl hit the ground, Kristen and Bridget immediately jumped up, not to celebrate but to make sure none of the front line of Alavarez took offense or and[**delete word] any type of swipe at Vanessa. Who having softly descended back to the ground stood there with a blank look on her face. It was the kind of look of a man who shot in self defense, the kind of feeling her father had explained to her when he was in the Desert war. Vanessa didn't want to hit the girl, but she had to.

The celebration began when the back fielders, including Janie, jumped the frontline, tackling them. The coaches shook hands as they both made their way to the downed LA girl. She was coming to and, aside from spitting a little blood from her cheek rubbing her braces, she was fine.

Bobby and Keith had been watching from the Grandstand and had just stopped celebrating. Keith turned to Bobby and said, "If you ever hear them start yelling Latin we just duck." Bobby shook his head in acknowledgment as they bounded down the stairs. They wanted to get out of there before the Kelly's saw Bobby. Bobby did not want the Kelly's to gather any suspicions about their relationship.

After a minute of celebrating back on the court the girls on both sides shook hands.

One of the Alavarez girls stopped Vanessa and asked, "The truth shall set you free?"

Janie leaned past Vanessa, and pulling her and Vanessa together said, "Consider us the Truth."

Vanessa finished the sentence with "And you're free. BYE BYE!"

Both Janie and Vanessa were slowly removing themselves from the slow motion which seemed to be in effect since the point started. Just as they were about to get back on the bus things finally went back to feeling normal for the two of them. Rhonda walked up to the girls and said to Vanessa, "Rebel Rebel Her face was a mess. Rebel Rebel How could they know Hot shot I loved it so." Immediately after she ran over to Ms, Hill and continuing her musical quotes told the coach, "Do you know I was born a Rebel?"

"I bet I know the place and day?" Ms. Hill said as she put her arm around Rhonda and they entered the bus.

Janie and Vanessa were getting back on the bus when Kristen walked up to them. Though she hated to admit it, she turned to them and said, "That was the greatest point I have ever seen."

Vannessa said thanks. "Hey, maybe no practice during game week is a good thing," pointing out how they were not able to practice since the game was so early.

"I will bring that up when I am Captain," Kristen said, looking to see if her new mythical play had given Vanessa the desire to run the team.

She was glad to see that it did not seem that way for now as Vanessa replied, "Good luck getting Ms. Hill to agree with that."

And as they were getting on the bus Kristen, not wanting to give all the glory to Vanessa, said to Janie, "Damn girl, maybe you can set ME like that sometime."

Things Are Different Now

Wednesday morning didn't seem different to Janie, as she rose and readied for school. She threw on her blue jeans and a green shirt that she had bought with her mom the week before. Summer was getting closer and closer and a jacket was no longer required or needed at all. Janie loved hoodies from Aero and Abercrombie and Fitch, and was doing her best to cope with wearing them less. She contemplated wearing one today, but it was supposed to be in the 70's. Janie loved knowing the hood was there to throw over her head and hair when she wanted to disappear from the world. For the last two weeks, Janie had wanted to disappear when she was at school. Janie thought it was ironic that the more her schoolmates ignored her, pretending she wasn't there, the more Janie wished she could comply and really just disappear.

Janie was out of breath as she raced to catch the Q31. As she got on the bus, she looked at her history report that she dropped while running for the bus. Such mad dashes for the bus were nothing out of the ordinary for Janie either. They were basically a daily ritual. Most of the regular drivers of the route, would usually look down Pigeon Meadow Road as they passed to see if she was sprinting for the bus. Timeliness was not one of Janie's strong points, but Just in Timeliness was and she rarely missed a bus. In fact, the last bus she missed was a cross town bus in Washington D.C. but that was the fault of Bobby's poor scheduling.

It wasn't until she stepped inside BA that things started to seem different. Amanda was by Tom's locker as she was every morning, chatting with him as he shoved his sports gear in it and grabbed his text books. At first Janie didn't react, as she walked by both Tom and Amanda said, "Hi."

Janie kept walking another five feet before she realized they were talking to her. She stopped and turned and almost had to get their attention again as she responded, "Hello." They both waved and Amanda smiled a little. Janie was not happy with her choice of hello, but she was really not prepared to greet anybody. Her being prepared or not didn't matter because by the time she made it to her locker, she had been greeted by at least another twenty kids and teachers.

Janie had no idea that Vanessa had called Kristen and pleaded to her future captain that they get out the word that Janie was a changed girl. Vanessa convinced her it would be best for the BA Rebels to make Janie as happy as possible. Kristen agreed in part to take any of the spotlights that Vanessa herself would receive from her magnificent play the night before.

Vanessa had no idea how quick Kristen, with the help of Amanda, could turn things around and was almost as surprised as Janie to see her homecoming. She stood in awe by her locker which was only a couple away from Janie's. Vanessa watched as Janie worked her way through the admiring crowd. Janie even had Principal Chambers come up to her and congratulate her on the shot.

"Ms. Hill told me about the play," he said. "She wants me to email parents to see if any of them recorded it. Must have been some point."

Vanessa had already given a play by play of "The Cuspis" to dozens of kids. Vanessa had tagged the point "The Cuspis" herself, feeling it added legacy to the play. As best as Vanessa could tell, cuspis was the word for point in Latin. Vanessa had actually called Janie last night as she did not really remember anything from the play herself. After getting a full breakdown of it, Vanessa added a few details herself before tagging it with the Latin word for point. Vanessa had also told Janie about her problems with Keith. They had been dating for a month now, and though he always hugged and kissed her lightly, they had yet to really kiss. Janie assured Vanessa that it was not her, and that Keith really loved her. "It will come at the right time," Janie said. "The first real kiss is important, and Keith is probably just waiting for the right time."

By third period, Janie was pretty sick of talking to people and was almost missing the silent treatment she was getting up to yesterday. The rest of the day settled down in excited greetings, and Janie realized how much she really did miss being part of the class. She decided she might even join another group in school. Janie had often done artwork for plays and decided she might officially join drama club.

Things were moving just as fast for Janie outside of school, as the four had agreed to meet today after school to see if they could figure out if the strange area was at the core of Janie's ability. As usual, they met at Dominique's. Bobby had gotten there early, ordering a roast beef sandwich. He was taking a big bite of it as the others pulled up in Keith's car.

"Looks good," Keith yelled out as he honked the horn to get Bobby's attention. A woman, insulted by the remark, assumed it was directed at her and huffed as she walk through the in-door of Dominique's.

Vanessa, seeing the woman, gave a little dig into Keith, "Keep your eyeballs in your head."

"I was talking about Bobby's sandwich!" Keith blurted out, thinking Vanessa was serious.

"Sure you were," giggled Janie from the backseat as Bobby came walking over. "It looks hot," Janie said, looking at Bobby's sandwich and laughing.

"It is," Bobby responded through a chew. "This place is the best." Bobby jumped in the backseat and gave Janie a peck on the lips.

"Eww," Janie said, "onions."

"And peppers," Bobby added as he blew towards Janie. Janie fanned and looked annoyed as Keith pulled away. Keith didn't want anybody seeing his car as they snooped around the special spot, so they parked outside the back gate. The area, and cemetery for that matter, seemed empty. There was no one around as far as they could see as they started taking down names on the tombstones. Janie gave them a general area that she suspected was the spot the strange people would visit. They all took out notebooks and started to write down the names and dates of the people on the different tombstones. Bobby had told them they could research the people at his house over the weekend and maybe find something that would let them know who they were trying to contact.

They were all still on their first sections when they heard the car pull up. As Janie looked a strange woman stepped out of the passenger seat of a small black car. Janie had seen her so many times from afar but was quite surprised to find the lady much younger than she believed. Janie realized now that her assumption of the lady's age was probably based on the style of clothes she wore. The woman was in a 70's style patterned dress with lots of beads around her neck. She waited by the car as the driver, a very large man, struggled out of his seat and joined her. The man was huge, in a black suit that looked like it was being quite taxed to keep all of the man within its material.

They both started to move towards the kids as Janie nervously moved toward where Bobby and Keith were writing stuff down. The whole group had heard the doors slam, and seeing Janie's reaction knew that this must be the woman. The lady ran her hand through her wild curly red hair as she got closer to the group.

"Don't you kids have some school to be at?" the lady asked in a very nasty tone.

"School's over," Keith said, trying to show he was not scared by the woman.

"So is your fun here. Now go!" she said, as she motioned to the man, who had finally labored his way to the group. He slid back his jacket and the kids could see that his journey out of the car and walk to the group had caused his shirt to come untucked. After he pushed back his shirt, the four saw the gun which was tucked into the man's belt strap.

"Make sure you don't come back. Do you understand me?" the woman added as she stood next to the man to make sure that the kids saw the gun.

The boys, who were bookending the girls as they stood, stepped forward and shielded their girlfriends as Bobby pointed to the back end of the cemetery and said to the lady, "We don't want any trouble."

"Well then, don't come back," the man said, releasing his jacket and letting it and his shirt flap once again to cover the gun.

They all quietly headed the way Bobby had pointed. No one said a word until they were through the gates of the cemetery.

"Was that real?" Bobby asked, directing his question at Keith.

"How the heck would I know," Keith responded. "It looked real, and he doesn't seem like the kind of person that would be walking around with a toy gun."

"I am pretty sure it was real," Vanessa interrupted. "I do not know the name but I have seen that gun before. My dad is a big collector. He keeps them in storage at the gun club he belongs to, but I believe he has one very similar. I am pretty sure he once told me it packs quite a punch for its size."

They continued to walk and turned a corner till they felt they were completely out of sight. Janie, who had not said much the entire time, sat down on the curb. No one had looked at anyone during the walk, and though the boys had taken their girl's hands before leaving the cemetery, it was only now that Bobby noticed the lack of color in Janie's face. Janie was still sitting quietly on the curb when Bobby knelt down next to her and asked, "Janie, are you okay? You look real pale."

"I'm okay, but I felt a strong feeling over there, and not just when that crazy lady pulled up. The whole time, you know, as we were looking at the tombstones. It was almost like my ears were ringing, and when the guy flashed the gun I thought my head was going to explode. I have to draw a caricature over there. I am not sure what or with whom, but I am drawing something important at that spot."

"No you're not," Bobby said sternly. "Not with some guy flashing a gun at us. We have to go to the police."

Keith had been wiping the tears away from Vanessa's eyes as Bobby was talking. Vanessa was leaning against a silver SUV, and Keith motioned to her to take a seat next to Janie and give her hug. As she did, Keith started making his way back to the cemetery.

Janie was continuing to plead with Bobby about going back, even as she was agreeing with him that it was too dangerous. Vanessa kept quiet, just rubbing Janie's arm hoping to warm her up and get a little color back in her face. In a few seconds Keith came jogging back from the cemetery.

"We have to do something. I need to figure out what this is all about," she said. "I don't think I will be able to sleep at nights if I don't figure out what's going on and why this is happening." Janie finished her plea.

Keith caught his breath and then jumped in over the others saying, "Well, maybe that's a good thing." Referring to Janie's comment about not being able to sleep. "'Cause I say we work the graveyard shift one last time," he added as he held up the lock from the back gate entrance. "You think we can find a twin for this?" Keith asked Bobby.

Bobby and Keith studied the lock and agreed that finding a duplicate and exchanging it would not be hard. Then, when they locked the cemetery at night, they would be snapping closed the replacement lock. Bobby snapped a picture of it and agreed to meet Keith tomorrow to check local hardware stores in hopes of finding a twin.

The girls were about to leave, but Bobby told Keith to drive them home as he was fearful of leaving the girls unguarded on the walk home.

Another Midnight Call

Bobby and Keith had no problem finding the lock as the first hardware store they walked into had an exact match. It was a hardware store a block from the cemetery, and when the owner was not too close, Bobby pointed out to Keith that the cemetery probably bought their lock here. They called the girls to meet them at Bobby's and in the Wu's backroom they laid out the plan. It would all start Friday afternoon; Bobby would quickly ride by the back gate and swap the lock they bought for the lock from the cemetery.

The caretaker seemed to always leave it open attached to the chains that were used to lock up the back entrance. Bobby would call or text and let the group know that the lock had been replaced and the mission was on for Friday night. The plan from there was to meet up at 11:45. The late meeting was required in order to not be detected in the cemetery. Janie tried to convince Bobby he did not need to go, and risk another long punishment, but Bobby refused to not be there. Keith and Vanessa also stated that neither planned to miss the chance to help Janie or the excitement of the mission. Janie could feel that the bond between the group seemed to have grown stronger since the threat from the man and woman. They all had built a sense of urgency to find out what was happening as soon as possible. Janie, being at the root and medium of the occurrence, seemed to always be looked at for approval of any of the ideas in the planning. She seldom objected to anything the group thought up, but it didn't seem to be set till she reiterated the idea to everyone.

In turn, the closeness of the group seemed to be causing changes to Vanessa that alone she never would have been strong enough to make. Since Vanessa and Janie's renewed friendship, Vanessa seemed to be drifting from her high profile position within the Prim and Proper. Kristen had finally convinced Amanda that maybe it was time to find another member of the grade's elite just in case Vanessa completely bolted from the group. Amanda agreed and often had Rachel join the lunch table. This was a good thing for the P&P, for the very next day, Thursday, Vanessa decided to lunch with Keith and Janie so they could talk about the midnight adventure. Amanda quickly made sure the school was aware that the seating re-arrangement was at her and Kristen's wishing and that they were not being dissed in any fashion by Vanessa.

Meanwhile Keith and the girls sat around one of the small tables that were near the food line. Keith filled them in on Bobby having bought them all flashlights and writing pads, and it was all ready to go in the backseat of Keith's car. They discussed tactics on how to go unnoticed as they entered the cemetery. Vanessa joked, asking Janie if she anything black to wear. Keith also let them know that he and Bobby went by the cemetery last night and was surprised to see quite a few lights at night within the cemetery. "It looks like some people are putting out solar lamps, this should really help us be able to use flashlights within the cemetery and go unnoticed," he said.

"I wish we had some light in the DC," Janie said. "Believe me, it's pretty scary at night. I am not looking forward to walking into the middle of Calvary tomorrow night." Janie made sure to keep her voice low so that other tables would not hear her.

By the time lunch had ended one of the girls from Vanessa's homeroom came up to her saying how sad she was to hear that Amanda decided to have Rachel replace Vanessa in the lunch group. Vanessa was fine with the rumors of her demotion; she knew the P&P was no longer for her. Janie and Vanessa were at the entrance to the cafeteria as Vanessa turned around to take one more look at table number one. Kristen and Rachel seemed to be commenting on Donna Sharon's outfit while Amanda was pretending to upchuck from disgust.

"Was I like that?" Vanessa asked, hoping for Janie to lie to her or somehow lessen the extent of her past actions.

"Not on the inside," Janie answered.

"Does that matter?" Vanessa asked, hoping for reassurance from her best friend.

Janie thought about it for some time and answered honestly, "Not really." Seeing that Vanessa was upset by the answer she quickly added, "But you're not like that any more inside or out and that all that counts."

The bell ending lunch rang just as Janie grabbed Vanessa's arm. Two minutes later the bell would ring again and you almost had to hurry to make it from the lunchroom to Mr. Kinear's trigonometry class.

Keith gave them both rides home on Thursday. Then on Friday, they again all piled into Keith's car but this time headed to Bobby's house, where they discussed final plans for their late night visit. They all headed home for dinner saying they would see each other later.

It seemed like Janie was in her room forever. She was about to draw a little but then became afraid anything she did now might influence the planned midnight caricature. She was pacing in her room for almost a half an hour when Janie glanced over at the clock. It was about 10pm. Her mom usually called it quits around that time and her father would usually watch the news for a little while and then follow suit. Janie decided that she should stop pacing and be as quiet as possible. Running out of options, Janie stayed awake by reading her book for English Class. She listened for her dad who went up to to his room about 11:15. That was about fifteen minutes ago and Janie decided she would finish the chapter before making a break for it.

After carefully monitoring her parents' room for some time, Janie crept down the stairs, glancing at the clock on the microwave. 11:40 was a little later than she had wanted, and she knew the others would be waiting for her. Janie's assumption about the others quietly lying in wait was correct as she counted three heads in Keith's car that idled as she approached it. Janie made it to the car and quietly opened the door. She didn't really need to be so quiet , as they were quite far from any house. Keith pulled away and drove. A half block from the back end of the cemetery he parked and shut off the lights. They all sat there quietly in the car until Bobby broke the silence and said, "Remember, try to move fast and no talking till we are well inside the gates."

Keith went first and unlocked the gate. He quickly loosened the chain and slipped in, waiting to the left of the gate by a small monolith that they all agreed to meet behind. One by one they darted in through the gate that Keith left slightly open. Bobby, the last person in, pushed the gate together and locked the gate back up.

Keith picked up the lantern which he had turned off as they all crouched down behind the monolith and assessed their entering. Nobody saw them was the general conclusion, and they quickly discussed the best way to get to the area. Bobby switched on the light on his compass watch and took the lead. After they got a good 100 yards into the cemetery, things got quite dark. Keith was reluctant to turn on the lantern, saying it might cause them to get caught.

"I don't want to fall into a dug grave," Vanessa said, imploring for Keith to light their way.

Keith continued to protest using the light, but as they marched further into the cemetery the more Vanessa filled with fright. The flags that were laid out at the tombstones seemed to have the most effect on her. The wind would fill them with air and make them jut out at them in the appearance of arms and legs. Each one they passed would cause Vanessa to almost pull Keith's arm out of its socket.

Finally, in an effort to save his arm from being completely ripped off, he set it for the dimmest level. Janie and Bobby were kind of getting familiar to walking cemeteries at night and the light wind and rustling of trees and flags had no effect on them. Vanessa, however, even with the added light, was still not comfortable with it and continued to clutch Keith's arm with every noise she heard.

It took them a while to get near the site, and all their eyes were getting better at dealing with the little amount of light the lantern was emitting.

"This is it," Janie whispered excitedly when they finally arrived at the location where the lady would frequent.

There were three main aisles in the area so everyone but Janie took an aisle. They pulled out the mini flashlights and pads and started writing down names and dates of the people on the markers. The flashlights were not very powerful but allowed them enough light to easily read the markers while hopefully not being noticed by anyone outside the cemetery.

Janie took out a pad from the knapsack she was wearing. She sat there for some time and then suddenly she began to draw. The glow of the lantern was not very strong, but between it and the moon Janie was able to see the pad slightly.

Janie stayed very quiet as the other were scurrying from tombstone to tombstone writing down everything on them, occasionally making fun of a name or attempting to pronounce one.

Vanessa whispered loud enough for the group, "This one has your initials. Maybe that's the catch."

"Yes, initials are very big in the afterlife," Keith said sarcastically and a little louder than he should. He lowered his tone and continued, "Just keep writing down names, whiz boy will find the common denominator on his computer."

"I don't think I will need to," Bobby said. "Janie, stop drawing. Guys, come here!"

They all made their way to the tombstone from which Bobby had been writing down facts.

"Alex Stratton." Keith read the name on the tombstone, but it did not ring a bell to Janie. He continued, changing the standard numerical dating into proper months, "Born February 2nd, 1963 to April 20th 1991."

"What?" Janie said. "That's…"

"Your birthday," Bobby and Vanessa said together.

"WOW," Janie and Keith commented in unison as well.

"Kill the light," Bobby interrupted. "I think something is driving in the cemetery." Bobby pointed to a moving light that seemed to be floating through the cemetery. Soon they all were able to make out that it was a large van, and definitely coming straight at them; though straight involved a few zig zags due to the way the road was built. There was a small row of bushes next to a mausoleum. Vanessa and Keith ducked behind the bushes while Bobby and Janie ran around to the other side and found similar matching bushes.

"Nobody say a word or move a muscle," Bobby yelled out a last order before everyone fell silent.

Janie's empty knapsack and the lantern remained in the middle of the aisle right where Keith had left it after turning it off. Keith thought about running out and grabbing them but the van was too close by that time. Bobby and Janie were much further from the aisle with the objects, and Janie, who wanted to finish her drawing, continued to sketch as they were hiding.

The van stopped right by the aisle, and Warren, the site's caretaker, exited the van. He turned on his flashlight which almost immediately hit the objects the kids had left in the aisle. After shining his light in a circle around the objects, Warren cautiously walked over to them. The days of tomb robbers had passed, but the freaks that he would occasionally find in the cemetery could be just as frightening and dangerous. The last person he ran into was a homeless man who threatened to put a curse on the cemetery. The caretaker thought it was ironic putting a curse on a cemetery, but the very next day they found out that someone had been buried in the wrong plot. It was just about the biggest pain in the cemetery business from the excavation to the amount of paperwork that had to be done. He approached the bag slowly and was relieved to see it was a knapsack. "Pranky kids," he thought. "Good, they don't usually spew curses."

"What do we have here?" he said aloud. "Seems like we have some people trying to get into the cemetery without having traveled the River Styx. Well, I have news for you, Zeus and the boys and girls on the mountain call me Charon." He picked up the lantern and illuminated it to the max. The man was wearing jeans and a custodial top that had a Calvary Cemetery red patch under the lip of the pocket that really stuck out on the olive drab shirt.

Both sets of kids were well hidden behind thick low bushes, but the pressure was mounting that sooner or later someone would be found. They wouldn't be heard for sure because the caretaker was almost making enough noise to wake the resting, as he went on about how teens should respect the dead or just respect anything. "How did respect get lost in the shuffle?" he asked aloud. "Why does your generation just think about themselves? Was it our fault?" Warren asked his unknown guests. "Alas poor Yorick," he said raising his hand up.

Vanessa was at the breaking point, it was this type of long winded bantering that drove her crazy about adults. This ongoing, know all "la la la" type talk just infuriated her, especially when it was loaded with references that she did not understand. When Vanessa got mad, action was taken, and she quickly thought of all the possible outcomes. What was truly important, she concluded, was that Janie be allowed to finish the drawing. She was part of a team, and she knew sometimes you had to take the hit so the other teammate could grab the flag. She ruffled Keith's hair, untucked her blouse, grabbed Keith and kissed him as she pulled some bushes. She actually made enough noise that it could even be heard over the caretaker's voice, as she and Keith shared their first long kiss. For a while Vanessa forgot about shaking the bush as their kiss became more intimate, but she had already made enough noise that soon the caretaker moved his flashlight in the direction of the bushes. As he got closer, he could start to see that his visitors were a young couple making out in the bushes.

"You know, the park is probably a less spooky place for lovebirds to coo," Warren suggested, as he shined the flashlight directly on the couple.

The word coo and the bright lit interruption of their first kiss, though expected, annoyed Vanessa further, and she responded angrily, "We were hoping for a little privacy." Vanessa started to get up and fix her shirt, making sure the caretaker saw her efforts. She was overselling now, but the idea of her being caught with Keith making out in a cemetery suddenly became a popularity thing. When the kids at school heard, she would be legend status; the instance might even get naming status, she thought to herself. Keith got up as well and brushed some imaginary dirt off his side as he started to fix his hair. He was still a little overwhelmed by the sudden kiss. Moving slowly, he grabbed a branch and freed himself from it as he rose. Keith continued to fiddle with the bush as he slowly awoke from the fog of Vanessa's passionate kiss. The kiss, their first real kiss, was also Keith's first real kiss. Though when he came to New York he was the mythical California Surfer demigod, in California he was the new kid from Vietnam who sounded funny. Though Keith talked a big game with Bobby and others, he had been scared to share that first kiss with Vanessa and was quite relieved to have gotten it over with.

As Keith fixed his shirt he realized the key to the gate was in his shirt pocket. As the caretaker continued to lecture them, Keith handed the key to Vanessa. He knew that somehow she would come up with a plan to get the key to Bobby and Janie.

Vanessa held the key for a second before she became conscious of what it was. "Thank you," she said, interrupting the caretaker's soliloquy and while winking to

Keith, acknowledging that she was aware of what needed to be done. Vanessa continued, "Yes, thank you Sam, for letting me introduce you to Uncle Alex. OH, how I miss him; how I miss him so much. And to go so young, well, well at least he went out on top. Yes, that is the key." Vanessa paused long enough for Bobby and Janie to soak in what she said. Feeling she had waited long enough for them to get it, for good measure she repeated the instructions a second time. "Yes, that's the KEY, the KEY to go out is on top. Oh poor Uncle Alex!" and she hugged Keith, pushing him up against the tombstone and laying the key on top of it.

The caretaker, having felt he had given them enough of a lecture, and not really wanting to hear any more about Uncle Alex, turned to Keith and Vanessa and said, "Okay, let me get you to the front gate, so I can open the cage and set you two little lovebirds free."

Keith, speaking for the first time since being ousted from the bushes, asked, "You mean you're not going to bust us?"

"No," answered the man briefly, being tired of talking.

"You caretakers are alright," Keith said as Vanessa looked slightly disappointed.

"Truth is, if I bust you, it's an hour before the cops come here and another half hour before they drag your parents down. I'm tired, I want to go to sleep. If some wacky lady didn't call me, I would have never even made my way over here. I mean, I can't even figure how the lady got my number. By the way, how did you get in here?"

"Oh, we hid when you locked up," Vanessa quickly responded, not letting Keith attempt to have to come up with a lie.

Warren directed them with his flashlight to walk in front of him as they all headed off to the van, which still had its engine running. Bobby and Janie continued to hide as Bobby peered out to watch the van pull away with Keith and Vanessa inside it. The entire time they were in hiding, Janie continued to draw. As the van disappeared into the darkness she had finished up the drawing. Bobby jumped up and grabbed the key atop of Alex's grave, and said to Janie, "Come on, we got to get out of here. I'm a little worried that the crazy lady might have been the crazy lady we ran into here the other day."

"Oh, I never thought of that," Janie said, as she closed her pad and started to run with Bobby. They stayed somewhat close to the fence of the cemetery gate so that they could see where they were going. They made it to the back gate fairly quickly. Bobby fumbled with the key for a second and finally got the lock unlocked. He loosened the chain, and he and Janie slithered through the gate. He tightened the chain back up and relocked the gate with the original lock that the caretaker had left out in the morning. He met Janie by the car as they noticed the caretaker's van turning the corner. They hid behind a SUV, as the caretaker let the lovebirds out by Keith's car.

After the van pulled away Janie started singing, "Vanessa and Keith sitting in a tree K-I-S-S-I-N-G."

"More like sitting in Poison Ivy," Vanessa said. "Are we done, because I am getting eaten alive and I am sick of looking at tombstones. Did you finish it?" Vanessa looked at Janie.

"Almost, but I can't show it to you. Not yet, I am not sure what it means," Janie said defensively.

"Hey, I didn't do all this not to see the pretty picture," Vanessa raised her voice.

"Keep it down," Bobby quietly whispered. "When she's ready, she will show it to us."

Janie tucked her pad back into her knapsack as they all hopped into Keith's car. Keith took Janie home first. She had left the back door unlocked when she snuck out. She quickly made her way back into the house. She quickly and very quietly locked the door.

She sat down at the kitchen table, took out the pad, and studied it for some time. Janie had no idea of why she drew what she did nor what it might mean. She waited a while till she was sure that no one was awake from her entering. She quietly crept upstairs and texted Bobby.

"You get inside okay?" her message read.

"Ye" came a reply. Janie shut off the phone not caring if Bobby sent a followup text that read "s".

Janie felt overwhelmed in the cemetery. Of all the caricatures she had done, none seemed to affect her like this. Janie had thought this last drawing would answer all her questions. Yet it really answered nothing, and as she lay in bed unable to sleep she began to weep. Although she entered the cemetery in a group Janie couldn't feel more alone as she wept in hope of an answer till she finally fell asleep.

Veritos Vos Liberat

Before Janie knew what hit her in the morning, she was in the car and on the way to guitar practice. Her phone was dead when she woke up, and she was not able to get a charge in it before her and her dad left the house. Janie would not have been able to talk about last night anyway, and she was extra careful what she texted, afraid her dad might have security settings on her phone. When your dad works for the phone company, Janie always said, you can never be too careful.

As she bounded down the stairs Janie could feel her legs were heavy, both from her late night adventure and her inability to fall asleep with so much still unanswered. However, this weakened condition did not stop Janie from really surprising Stan when she started playing at her lesson. It had been almost a month since they last met, and Janie had improved dramatically. Stan looked confused as Janie breezed through the first three songs that Stan selected. Stan did not know that for much of the time since their last lesson Janie had been locked in solitary confinement. During that time, her guitar and books were the only entertainment she had. Choosing anything above reading a book, Janie had even taught herself a new song from a Green Day guitar music sheet she had gotten in her stocking for Christmas. Janie played them while Stan pointed out techniques to speed up a couple of the chord changes.

Stan proudly ended the lesson saying what a nice jam it was. Janie raced to the car, scaring her dad as she rapped on the window. As usual her dad was reading the paper and listening to the Sports talk station. He almost spilt his coffee as Janie jumped into the front seat.

The car ride seemed to take three times as long as usual as Janie tapped her foot impatiently to the songs on the radio. Mr. Kelly finally pulled the car into the driveway. Janie jumped out of the Ford Fusion right as it stopped moving. She had already entered the house by the time Mr. Kelly had gotten out of his seat. Janie flew up the stairs like she knew her phone was ringing. The phone was shaking on her desk like a wet Chihuahua, but by the time she got to it, the phone had stopped its mad dance. The whole guitar lesson, she was worried that one of her nightshift partners might have sent a text, with a little too much information for comfort.

She fired up her computer as she checked her phone with her other hand. Five texts and three messages had come in. "How in the world did I survive the two and a half weeks without my phone," she thought. "It's like a part of one's being." She even contemplated for a couple of seconds which she missed more, the phone or Bobby. Quickly she realized that Bobby was 71% of her calls. The phone simply could not be missed more, for it relied too much on Bobby to be compared to him.

Janie checked and five of the messages were from Bobby. She quickly did the math and realized it came to 62.5%. She would have to re-address her Bobby / phone missing scenario later, as 71% was obviously too high a percentage.

She started to look through the texts. All three of Bobby's texts put together made the sentence, Janie you have to call me ASAPP. Janie tried to figure out what the second "P" might have stood for if Bobby had actually meant to

195

include it. "Pretty, Poopy, Pal, Peewee, Possum." She decided to go with Pretty.

Vanessa had also called to discuss her first real kiss with Keith and left a two minute message about it. How magical it was, even if it was to keep the others from getting caught. Vanessa was even more excited as, after they dropped Janie and Bobby off, they shared kiss number two. She also asked Janie about the picture, but Janie replied that the picture wasn't finished. It actually was done, but she still didn't want to show anybody. For one she wasn't nuts about the way it came out. In her defense, she drew half of it in the dark while sitting in a bunch of bushes. More importantly, she still did not understand what it meant. She tried to stop thinking about it and went back to thinking up P nicknames, Punjab, party, parrot, Parakeets, Parka.

Suddenly her phone started to vibrate in her hand. It was Bobby.

"What's up, pelican," she said.

"What's up pelican what?" Bobby replied, not really sure to what Janie was referring to.

"You made a PP on my phone," Janie giggled.

"Janie, we got to talk," Bobby said, as he was used to often talking over the nonsense that he did not understand.

"Okay, Pooh bear," Janie giggled.

"Janie, stop. I am serious, I did some research this morning. I got to talk to you," he said in a tone that finally got Janie to be serious.

"Shoot." Janie stopped joking, realizing Bobby's somber mood was not about to change.

"No, in person, I got to see you."

"Okay okay. You want me to come by, I will catch a ride with my mom." Janie glanced over at the Cheshire Cat faced clock that hung above her door.

Bobby paused for a moment to consider Janie's suggestion and then replied, "It might be better, in case you want to see what I pulled up. My dad has access to some online databases through work. I have been playing with them lately, especially pulling information about the people we have visited. Well, I found some stuff about Alex. I need to talk to you about it, but you might want to see it."

"Okay, I will come by. I think my mom is leaving in half an hour. I will see you then penguin," Janie said, once again confusing Bobby as they said goodbye.

Janie checked her computer and saw the wonderful news. "Lah Lah Lah" was No. 12. "Goodbye E££ia," she said aloud. "Oh thank God, go back to your drinking and partying and just stop making music."

It was getting near the end of the school year. The homework was getting lighter, though there were a couple of projects that were due on the horizon. That is, if the horizon was next week. She picked up the science library book and started to write down facts on fuel cells in her notebook. She was partnered with Rhonda on a project about alternate fuel sources. She got about a half a page done by the time she was about to leave. Her mom was putting on her earrings as she entered Janie's room. "Are you ready, honey?" she asked.

197

"All set." Janie looked at her mom and took one more look at the Cheshire Cat. She had been dying to tell her about Bobby since Washington and for some reason, now seemed like the right time. "Mom, Bobby and I are Boyfriend Girlfriend."

Mrs. Kelly's earring slipped right out of her hand as she and Janie watched it roll under the bed. Both mother and daughter were a little scared to look at each other. Though the confirmation was earring dropping material, Mrs. Kelly was not completely shocked. Just yesterday she and Mrs. Wu had discussed the exact possibility. "My little girl is dating. And what's more she told me," she thought to herself while she picked up the earring. Evelyn couldn't be happier. Bobby was a great, smart, and respectful kid. Mrs. Kelly walked over to her little girl, and hugged her. Janie was in tears, and it had spread to her mom as they hugged and wept.

"Mom, you can't tell Mrs. Wu. Bobby doesn't know I told you yet." She looked at her mom, as her mom shook her head yes. Janie continued, "And not dad either, Mom, will he be upset?"

"Upset?" Janie's mom laughed. "He loves Bobby. I think he might be the only boy that would not upset him. It will scare him plenty though." Mrs. Kelly laughed, as she released Janie and headed downstairs to the car.

Bobby was sitting on his stoop when Mrs. Kelly pulled up. Janie kissed her mom goodbye and ran up the front steps. Mrs. Kelly took a little longer than usual watching her daughter run up the steps. Bobby and Janie hugged politely, but Bobby, not knowing that the cat was half way out of the bag, didn't do more.

"What's up Pinocchio?" Janie asked remembering about Bobby's extra "P" once she saw him.

"Nothing Shipetto," Bobby instinctively responded, not really sure if he actually remembered his name correctly, or why they were making Disney cartoon references.

"So what do you want to show me? This better be good, because I have three projects to do." Janie could feel the storm of some heavy report work brewing, and today might be the last day of slacking off on them. Janie had no problems doing homework or chapter reading assignments, but when it came to doing projects, she always put it off. Once she started she would rarely stop until it was done, but starting the project was a chore she would put off.

They headed inside the house and went to the back library, saying hi to Mrs. Wu who was in the kitchen. Mrs. Wu was busy making Bobby a turkey sandwich and asked Janie if she would like one. "That would be wonderful," Janie replied, realizing she had not eaten since breakfast. Mrs. Wu's phone rang and Janie waited until she was sure it was not her mom.

"Pickle?" Mrs. Wu asked after she hung up the phone.

"Pickle!" Janie yelled, continuing her imaginary P game with Mrs. Wu. "Nice one."

Mrs. Wu looked at Bobby, who looked as confused as she was. Janie noticed their confusion and said, "Pickle would be lovely. Thank you."

They headed into the back room and by the time Bobby had booted up the computer, his mom entered with two turkey sandwiches and two cans of soda. Bobby grabbed the Sprite, leaving the Pepsi for Janie. "So are you ever going to tell me why I am here?"

"It's about Alex," Bobby said, right after his mom left the room and right before he took a bite of his sandwich.

"The guy from the cemetery?" Janie asked, though she was sure it was whom Bobby was talking about. She thought about taking out her pad and showing Bobby, but she decided not to. She took another bite of her sandwich, as Bobby pushed his aside as he got up from the computer chair he was sitting in and sat down next to Janie on the couch. He checked to make sure his mom was nowhere in sight and took Janie's hand. "Janie, Alex might mean more to you than you think. Janie, what I found, I am not really sure if I am right, but I think Alex may have died in the same hospital where you were born."

Janie pulled her hand away from Bobby. She wasn't mad at Bobby; she was just trying to deal with everything and holding Bobby's hand didn't seem to be resolving anything. "I suppose he died in the morning close to my birth."

Bobby gave up on trying to hold Janie's hand as he continued to fill her in on his research. "Yes, if I am right, there is more. Janie, first of all, Alex was a woman, not a man. Not just a woman, she was pregnant and giving birth at the time." Bobby went back to the computer and hit a couple of buttons. A newspaper article popped up about the incident. Janie went over and stood next to Bobby as she started to read it on the screen. Janie read about the hospital drama where the woman went into labor, but suddenly there were complications. It listed steps the doctors took and how they thought the child would not make it. The doctors were able to miraculously save the child but in the process the mother did not survive. Janie got through most of the article and felt she had read enough. She went back over and collapsed on the couch. She was getting annoyed about Bobby's snooping and didn't see any point in it. "So, she went the same day. Big deal, it happens every day."

"Janie, you need to hear the last paragraph of the article." Bobby hit the down arrow and a little more of the article appeared.

"Well[, go ahead Bobby, read it," said Janie, displaying her annoyance in her tone.

"The doctors tried for hours with the mother going in and out of consciousness, while other doctors worked on delivering the child. It was a good thing that there were no other deliveries at the hospital that night or morning."

"What are they talking about?"

"I checked other articles and sites as well. It seems like there was only one delivery in Wilkins that night and morning." He went to hold Janie's hand but she would have none of it. Janie didn't know what to think; she was so confused that she just got up and went through the back door into the Wu's yard. Bobby followed, but by the time he got outside Janie had already mounted Bobby's bike and was heading down his driveway. He wanted to yell something, but he didn't know what to say. He ran to the front of the house to make sure that Janie was okay, and she was already about half way up the block by the time he got there. Bobby thought about walking to her house, but it didn't seem like he would be of any help. He went back to his computer and sent Janie a text saying when she felt up to it to text or call him. He would be home waiting.

The ride from Bobby's was not far, yet it seemed like forever. Janie wasn't concentrating on biking at all. She almost lost her balance as she hit a large crack that she had avoided a million times before. Janie had to see her father. He needed to explain to her what was going on. The back gate was open as she pulled in the driveway and she rode Bobby's bike right up to the backdoor of the house without stopping. She could see her dad in the kitchen and she took a couple of seconds to catch her breath. Her dad was getting up from the kitchen table as she entered. "Dad, you need to explain it to me, so I understand," Janie said sternly.

"Explain what, honey?" her father said, going over to hug her. Only Janie really didn't want to be hugged, and her father realized something was amiss. He brushed her hair out of her eyes and tried again to give her a warm hug, but again, she wanted answers, and more than that, she wanted explanations.

"Dad, when I was born, there was a big commotion at the hospital. Did you see any of it?" Janie tried to sound nonchalant but the topic was so pointed that it was impossible to make it feel like small talk.

"What commotion?" Dad asked.

"Bobby and I were reading some article about a lady who passed away while giving birth. This was on the same morning I was born." Janie continued to fill her dad in on what she wanted explained.

"It wasn't chaos throughout the hospital, if that is what you mean. Doctors, lots of different doctors, would come in and out of the room. But you wouldn't know it outside, at least,

I don't think you would have," her father said about the situation Janie had read about.

"How do you know? Do you remember it, and were you and mom close by?" Janie looked right into her dad's eyes.

"I remember it quite well, Janie. I was in the room and so were you." He pulled out a kitchen chair away from the table for her to sit. "Janie, hopefully you will understand, but something like that day, you don't easily forget. Everything seemed to be going fine, we made it to the hospital in plenty of time. Your mother was pushing away and the doctor was brought in, because the delivery would be very soon. Then, ten minutes later he and the nurse start discussing something, and before I know it, a monitor being pushed by another doctor was rolled into the room. They all looked worried as they questioned the nurse who was helping with the contractions. I was just standing there, I knew that something was going wrong, but they didn't seem that concerned. I had no idea how truly grave it was, not at first anyway."

"What are you talking about? You were all in the room?" Janie asked her dad, trying to understand fully the situation her dad was describing.

"Yes, I was there because that woman who passed was your mother. It was horrible. All the time they thought we were going to lose you, and the doctors were scrambling. They told me later that your signs came back just as hers faded. The doctors did everything they could, they really did. After, one doctor, the one who really led the efforts, said he was sure you were not going to make it. I know this will sound weird but he continued telling me he almost felt like your mom offered up her life so that you would pull through."

203

Janie froze as she had pondered the possibility that her mom and Alex were the same. In fact, she felt a strong possibility when she hopped on Bobby's bike. When she left Bobby's she convinced herself that once she spoke to her dad everything would go back to normal. Only, that didn't happen, and now Janie just fell into a shocked like state. Hearing about her mom for the first time and all she went through, it was not easy for her to comprehend it all of a sudden in one moment.

Her dad looked solemn as he stopped talking. For a while he didn't move but just stood there next to the kitchen table. He wanted to hug her, and comfort her, but when he finally moved toward her she pushed out her hands keeping him at a distance.

"You can be mad and confused," her father said in a very soft voice.

"Don't tell me what I can be," Janie responded matter of factly. "Just tell me why."

"Janie, things like this are not easily explained by why. What happened that night will never leave me. Your mother and I were very much in love and only married for a couple of months before we found out you were on the way. We were so in love, but her dad, your real grandfather, he was not as happy with the situation." Janie convulsed when her dad mentioned her real grandfather, as opposed to the fake one whose lap she had fallen asleep on a million times.

"The doctors did everything they could. I was there when she took her last breath and you, your first. After that night, I went through quite of deal of counseling as I stayed in the hospital. You had to remain in ICU for weeks yourself. They tried to support your grandfather too, but he was inconsolable. He blamed me and worse, he blamed you for what happened. I tried to handle things with him however he wanted. He wanted to handle the funeral and everything, and I let him do whatever he wanted. He never changed; he just stayed angry at me and even worse at you. I am not making excuses for him but he had a very difficult time even before that night. His wife had left him many years before that night, she had just up and left him, taking their baby infant girl with her. Alex was all he had, and he blamed me and you for her death. For a year I tried to keep in touch with him, but my calls would go unanswered and the letters would come back unopened. During that year I met your…"

"Evelyn," Janie interrupted, not allowing him to say mother.

"Yes, I met Evelyn when you were about four months. I mean, she worked at the phone company, and I knew her before that a little. When we worked together she was very caring, and would often help me out. Her sister had two kids and Evelyn knew a lot from helping her." As her father paused she thought about Anne and Teresa whom he was referring to, her favorite cousins. Janie's world could not have been unwrapping faster.

"She took such great care of you, and soon we fell in love. I think she might have loved you before she loved me," he truthfully added, hoping that it would help ease Janie's state of mind.

"Then, she decided to make you call her my mother," Janie added

"It was my decision, I didn't want you to have to know the other story Janie. I am not saying I was right. I am only saying I was thinking about you when I made the decision. I always planned to tell you, but I think, I was just waiting for the right time. Really, I had always planned to tell you, but just wanted you to be old enough to understand," he said as he reached out to hold her again. This time she allowed his hug as she started to sob lightly. "Why were you looking this up?" her dad asked, hoping not to upset Janie with his curiosity.

Janie still had no desire to tell her dad about her powers. Well, her and her mother's powers to be more specific. Janie thought for a long time before she responded, "It's just, I would often walk by that way through the cemetery on the way home from school. As I walked past this one area I would always get this feeling, this strong feeling. Yesterday Bobby and I, we looked at the tombstones and we saw the one for Alex had the same date as my birthday. I don't understand, the last name says Shannon."

"Her father refused to have her buried with her married name. I agreed with anything to try to make him feel better. I was hoping he would want to be part of your life. We were only married for a less than a year..."]

"Dad, I want to stay here. Promise me we won't move. I want to be by her."

"I promise," her father said, as he hugged her.

Bobby was still in the backroom study. He was very concerned for Janie and had texted her. He didn't want to call and figured when Janie was ready, she would get in touch with him. Janie had left her knapsack on the couch. Bobby kicked it off as he spread his legs out on the couch while turning on his portable game console. He played Time Escape for about fifteen minutes but quickly became disinterested. As he got off the couch to get the newspaper from the living room, he noticed that Janie's drawing pad was in her bag. Bobby couldn't resist and sneaked a peek] at what Janie had drawn last night in the cemetery. It was an infant being held by two arms. Bobby knew exactly what it was all about and quickly put the pad back in the bag. He shuffled through the items on the desk and grabbed his cell. He again thought about calling Janie but did not want to rush her into a conversation.

Back at the Kelly's, Janie had heard enough from her dad and was crying uncontrollably as her dad consoled her. It continued for several moments when suddenly her mom bounced through the back door. "What's the matter?" Evelyn asked as she laid a grocery bag on the floor and walked over to the two. "It's not Bobby." She stopped herself, not sure if Janie had told her father.

"Mom," Janie said with no problem or hesitation. "I know, Bobby and I kind of figured it out, then dad told me the whole story. " She went over to hug her mom, who was still trying to digest what Janie was talking about. It didn't take her long to digest as the next words out of Janie's mouth were, "Don't worry, you will always be my mom, you have done so much for me."

Evelyn, hugging Janie, turned her head to Tom, who had a look of relief in his face. "Thank you, Janie," she said turning to face her again. "I love you so much, I can't begin to explain to you how much," she said as she began to cry. Janie hugged Evelyn tight and wept along with her.

"One thing," Janie looked at her parents, "I want to stay here by her." Janie repeated her earlier plea for confirmation.

Evelyn hugged her again, "Janie, we will never take you away from your mother. I promise." Tom grabbed the two of them and pulled them even closer together. They stayed that way for some time until Mr. Kelly said to Janie, "Let's go say a prayer for your mom." Evelyn stayed home as Mr. Kelly and Janie went to her mom's tombstone. Janie had not paid much attention to the tombstone the night they visited, as she had no idea of its importance.

It's Been a Long Time

"At first, I use to come in here quite a bit," Janie's father said. "As I would walk in, I often wondered if her father picked the location on purpose to upset me. It didn't work if he did. I would stop by all the time and give your mom updates of how you were doing. Sometimes for hours just telling her of all the amazing things that you were doing."

Janie's dad took a break from talking to wipe his eyes which had been filling up since they started their walk to reunite their true family. "I still come here now and then, but I've tried to go when you're not around. When you were little, really little, I used to bring you."

As they got closer to the tombstone, Janie tried to remember coming as a little girl, but she must have been too young. When they got there, they both said a prayer. Janie could feel her mom with her. She had been noticing of late that when she channeled, she felt cold but now she realized it wasn't as much cold as it was its own unique feeling. She just equated it to being cold because it caused her to move like she had a chill. She wanted so bad to see her and to be held by her rather than feel her this way.

Janie thought about telling her dad about the drawings, but was not sure if it would frighten him, and make him less inclined to allow her to visit the cemetery. With all the thoughts running through her head, Janie never noticed the car that was sitting parked close by at one of the intersections of roads within the cemetery.

It was the same car that the weird lady and giant of a man traveled in the last time when they confronted the group. It stayed parked with the driver inside the whole time while Janie and her dad prayed. After they finished, Janie gathered some dandelions and laid them in front of the tombstone. Her father said they would go out and pick up some real flowers to plant tomorrow.

He told how he paid for a package of flowers to be planted throughout the year. "But we can plant whatever you want, whenever you want," he added.

Janie insisted she wanted to go down to Paul's Flowers down the block and pick out something right now. Her father agreed. She told him that she was going to go herself, just wanting a little time to digest everything on her own. Mr. Kelly tried to protest for a second, but Janie convinced him that it would be best for her, and her father finally agreed.

They headed together out of the cemetery as her dad told her all sorts of things about her mom. There wasn't too much left to the mystery causing Janie's ability. Yet her father, unaware of Janie's powers, offered one more bit of enlightenment when he looked into Janie's eyes and said, "She was an artist, like you."

"She drew?" Janie asked, completely overwhelmed to hear her mom was a fellow artist, and helping her to understand a little more how she is able to draw the caricatures.

"She drew, sculptured and did murals; she was amazing." Her dad paused and added another, "Like you."

Janie and her dad hugged, as he gave her $20 and told her to bring home whatever plants she didn't use. "We'll plant them somewhere special in the back," he said.

Janie was a little surprised by the prices when she got to Paul's; still $20 was more than needed. She looked at all the different styles of flowers before settling on a multi colored flat of impatiens. When she returned back to her mom, the black car was still there, though a little more off in the distance. Janie took out a shovel she had grabbed from the house and started to dig. Janie put the pinks on the outside of the group and red and white in the middle. She completely overdid the amount of flowers, leaving only one of each color to bring home. They were butted so close together they looked like a head of broccoli, but Janie thought they were perfectly placed with every nook and cranny filled. Janie stood up and took a couple of steps back to admire her planting. Noticing a hose spigot, she found an empty water bottle and went back to work, watering the flowers. After three trips to the water spigot, the plants seemed to have been thoroughly drenched. Janie got up and took a few steps back to admire her work. Suddenly she felt a hand lay upon her shoulder. Turning around, she said, "Dad, what did you think?" Only it wasn't her dad.

"I thought I told you not to come back," the strange lady stepped forward as Janie moved back. They did this for a couple of steps until Janie was almost stepping on the flowers she just planted.

Janie was trying not to look into the lady's eyes as she did not want her to see how frightened she was. Believing that fear could not be sensed, thanks to Bobby and MIT, she went on the offensive. "Well, I am here, and you can't stop me," Janie said as she stopped stepping backwards. The lady still moved at Janie who could feel the backs of her sneakers sinking into the soft wet ground she just watered.

"Well, I am glad you did. I have something for you," the lady said, as Janie thought the lady was happy Janie had returned so she could finish her off. Janie took one last step backwards and her butt hit the tombstone. The lady reached into her jacket and Janie saw it as her only chance. She rushed the lady before she could get out whatever was in her pocket. Janie fell on top of the woman. As the lady hit the ground her hand fell out of her jacket pocket. Janie reached out and held the lady's hand away from her as she focused on the shiny object. Janie focused on the lady's weapon hand only to see the object was a cross.

The lady, beginning to shake from the rattling in her head from the fall, looked at Janie and yelled, "What are you doing?"

"You're not going to kill me?" Janie asked, still maintaining her control on top of the woman.

"What? No, I wasn't planning to," the lady said as she stopped struggling and went about pleading her case. "I never had an intention to harm you. My friend, I asked him to help me scare you and your friends away. I thought you kids were hooligans. I didn't know what I do now. You looked like a bunch of troubling kids that were up to no good."

Janie, sensing the lady was telling the truth, started to remove herself from on top of the lady. She got up quickly and watched the lady to make sure that she was not lying, so she could attack. She thought about helping the lady up, but was relieved to see by the time she was about to extend her hand the lady had half risen.

The lady nodded and waved her hand a little to show peace after she stood and continued talking. "As I was saying, Daniel, the rather large man you met, well I asked him to scare you. "

"Well, his gun did a pretty good job at that."

"He is a cop," the lady said. "He is also one of my clients. I happened to be doing a séance for him that day."

"Van-," Janie was about to let the lady know Vanessa had identified the gun type, but didn't mention anything about cops using them. Janie had stopped herself from mentioning Vanessa's name, not wanting to give the weird lady any information about any of the group. Besides, Vanessa didn't say cops do not carry that type of gun. Trying to get off the topic of Vanessa's name], Janie said, "Pretty large cop, I would have thought he was a bus driver."

"Yes, well," the lady responded before realizing it was not worth the effort to figure out the bus driver thing. She went on, "I asked him to scare you away, but it did more than that. It seemed to have scared my link away as well," she said, with a regret and tone in her voice that she did not have until now.

"Your link?" Janie was not sure whether to emphasize more "your" or "link," when she replied angrily. As she replied Janie fell into a jog of wonderment that there was someone] else that might be experiencing the same powers.

The lady acknowledged Janie's tone on both words and could tell she might have implied some form of ownership. "I mean, it is not mine, but somehow I am experiencing something. I cannot fully explain it to you, but there are people who are troubled, people who want so badly to speak to a loved one or someone who has passed. I help them, I think."

"You help them?" Janie asked, hoping the lady would go on.

"I think I do. I mean most of them come back to me later, and they tell me they feel better. They thank me. They tell me they feel like the message really got to the person."

Janie, for a half a second, almost wanted to tell her about her ability, but again, thought better of it and remained silent on the topic.

The lady again waited to make sure Janie did not want to say anything before she went on. "My whole life, I was a charlatan, telling people made up fortunes. I would just tell them what they wanted to hear, so they would give me what I wanted. For years, the same people, oh they would come and go. Sometimes, I guess they would wise up and leave for good, but not before I took them for a ride. Those rides, sometimes they went pretty far."

213

Janie was listening, but not completely sure why the lady was confessing to her. Janie was about to tell the lady she had to go home, as she was beginning to grow quite bored about hearing about her fake reading and how she ripped people off.

However, the lady, not allowing Janie to get a word in, especially goodbye, continued, "And then, I came here. I brought somebody here for the effect. But I knew it that day, when we were done, the man felt better. Maybe blind luck brought me here or maybe it was something more powerful, but the message I gave, it got through. Soon word spread, believe it or not, word does spread in the fortune teller circles. Soon, anybody who had to get a message to the other side, something that was eating at them; well, they came to me, and after they came they felt peace. They still pay me, though I don't take them for rides anymore. No, I help them, somehow, I am not sure how but somehow they feel it. They feel the message made it."

"Well, I'm glad for you. I have to go." Janie was annoyed slightly that her mom was being used to make money for this lady, even if it was helping people. She wanted to just leave the conversation and put this on the pile of things she had to digest in her mind.

"Before you go, I wanted you to know: all this stopped the day I threatened you and your friends. And I didn't feel the way I did before, until today again. Whatever I did, I upset the peace, and I am sorry. Here, I want you to have this. This was at the tombstone when I first came here." The lady handed her the cross and continued, "I promise I will not bother you anymore, and if I am here when you come. I will leave. I do not want to impose. I am sorry for trying to scare you off. I really thought you were a bunch of kids just up to no good."

Janie accepted the cross as she told the lady, "Thank you, Maybe we could work out some kind of schedule," Janie said, knowing it was a strange idea, but she just wanted to get away from the lady. As she took the cross from the lady, Janie noticed the lady had a very unique smell but Janie couldn't place it.

"So how did you know Alex?" The woman couldn't finish the statement before Janie answered.

"He was a family friend," Janie answered, not wanting to give away any information about her mom or their relation.

"Oh, well, I have to get going," the lady said, sensing Janie wanted her to leave.

"Me too," Janie said, glad at not having to be the one to break up the meeting.

Janie took one more look at the tombstone and departed quickly. She raced to Bobby's house while calling home on the way. She just wanted to let them know she was heading to Bobby's house so he wouldn't worry.

Her mom answered the phone. "Janie?" she said. She tried to sound the way she always sounded, but hung on the line, unsure if her voice sounded the same to Janie anymore.

"Hey mom," Janie said without hesitation, which made both feel wonderful. "I am heading over to Bobby's house. I want to see him quick. I will be home in time for supper."

"Okay dear," her mom replied.

"I love you," Janie said softly.

"Love you too," her mom replied, with tears in her eyes.

Janie knocked softly on the Wu's front door, and Bobby answered. He hugged her tightly on the stoop, not really caring if his mom was looking on. "You okay?" he asked.

"Yeah," Janie replied. "You were right. She was my mom."

"I had a feeling, I sneaked a peek at your drawing after you left," Bobby admitted, not wanting to lie to Janie.

They headed into the den, saying hi to Bobby's mom on the way. Janie let Bobby know everything that happened and showed him the drawing.

Janie went on to tell him about the crazy lady, and what they had in common.

"Bobby, I am sorry you and the others weren't there when everything went down. I almost feel like it was our adventure together," she said as she grabbed his hand.

"We knew eventually it was going to come down to something you were going to have to go through yourself. We were there to support you till you had to go alone," Bobby said. "Did you get her name? Maybe we can look her up on the web and find out what people say about her abilities."

"Bobby, you don't think she will be able to find out who Alex is?"

"There was no obituary," he said. "Not that I could find."

"I think because her last name might be Kelly." Janie said as she hugged him again.

Bobby's mom peeked her head into the back room. She tried to not notice that Janie and Bobby were breaking from a hug, and with a crack in her voice asked, "Would you kids like some Fritos or something?"

"FRITOS!" Janie yelled out.

Mrs. Wu looked at Bobby, and they shared another confused look similar to the morning's with each other.

Janie realized her outburst, and lowered her voice and said, "Fritos would be lovely."

As Mrs. Wu headed back into the kitchen, Janie excitedly told Bobby, "I forgot to tell you the weird lady had a strange smell. I just realized she smelled like Fritos."

"I am not surprised," Bobby laughed.

The Last Game and Day

The Regionals for The Rebels came quickly and were over even faster. The Rebels had to play the number one seed, Washington High, who were the defending champions. They were from Forrest Hills and the school was much bigger in enrollment than Bay Academy. Ms. Hill invited the cheerleaders for additional support, but neither the cheering nor Ms. Hill's motivational speech was able to get the team charged like when they battled Alvarez High. The

Rebels would have been completely destroyed had the Washington High's Sentinels coach played his starters throughout. It didn't matter to Ms. Hill; the principal had already told her that both herself and the team were back next year.

When the game was over Bridget handed her practice whistle to Kristen, and everybody, including Vanessa, cheered the official passing of command to her. That was until Kristen suggested some practices in the summer, which led to Rhonda screaming for a recount. Ms. Hill had to convince Kristen that if she wanted to keep the whistle, she wouldn't be blowing the whistle till next fall.

The rest of the school year moved very quickly as well. The drama team's play went off without a hitch, running for three nights to a sold out auditorium. Vanessa, thanks to her volleyball fame, actually landed a small talking role when one of the senior girls dropped out. The play, written by one of the students in Janie's class, was about some kids at a camp. Vanessa played one of the scared girls that were lost in the forest. The director was quite impressed with her acting, unaware of Vanessa's recent nighttime fright that was used for the basis of her performance.

Janie, for the first time, was in charge of designing and building all the set designs, with Keith aiding her as the assistant designer.

One of the camp scenes was a seaside, and Janie allowed Keith to have complete control of it. Although the two of them went over budget by $70 dollars, when the drama teacher saw the finished sets he was astounded and found the extra money.

Janie also managed to pull all her grades back to A's and once again was positioning herself to have the best grade point average of the grade. She could sense some competition from Keith for top student next year, but she knew that anytime it got close she could call a friend who would find a way to distract him from his school work. Being valedictorian was always a dream to Janie, and even with all the adventure and revelations she had been through, her desire to win it was still at tops of things she aimed to achieve.

Janie had often tried to figure out why she wanted to be it, but as of yet was unable to really understand why.

Janie, Vanessa and Keith ate lunch together every day. Janie had filled them in on that first Monday back about her mom and her run-in with the weird lady. They asked Janie if she minded that the lady seemed to be using her mom.

"I don't know, I mean I assume if she didn't want to help the lady she wouldn't," Janie said, not really wanting to discuss that aspect any more.

Sometimes talk would come up about what they should do, if anything, with Janie's gift in the future; who they could help or what they could solve. However, the last few days, the talk centered around the volleyball match between the four of them. It and the end of school was a day away, and Janie and Vanessa were jokingly smack talking Keith to rubble at lunch.

"I can't believe our parents are letting us go," Vanessa said to Janie, giving her boyfriend a break from the abuse.

"Keith, it was a brilliant idea to get them all together." Janie gave props to Keith, who had his dad have all their parents over for dinner last week.

Tomorrow's game was to take place at Jones Beach, and thanks to last week's dinner, all had been granted permission to go to the beach with Keith to celebrate the first day of summer vacation. The girls had claimed to do quite a bit of training in developing a secret weapon.

Keith would often argue with them, saying that he and Bobby didn't need a secret weapon to defeat two little girls. On the last day the smack talk continued all the way through the afternoon, and as they sat waiting for Ms. Freeman to start her last art class, Vanessa couldn't resist one more crack, saying, "Keith Dear, you will still open the car door for me after we whip you?"

"Yes, of course, and slam it before you get your long legs in," he replied.

The quiet before the storm is what an artist would most likely have named his piece if he was to paint Ms. Freeman's class as the bell signaled the start of the last class of the year.

"They say the passing of time is one of the hardest events to capture in art." Ms. Freeman interrupted Janie and Vanessa's conversation by walking over and talking to them. Ms. Freeman would usually interrupt disruptive classroom banter in this way. Not intentionally brushing off Vanessa, she continued to talk to her two favorite students. "So Frida and Diego, how would you capture our last minutes together? Time is passing, yet the clock doesn't seem to be moving at all. The inevitable things that lay ahead are just about to happen, how do you capture them when you can't draw time?" Ms. Freeman would often call Janie and Keith by famous artistic couples, sometimes calling them Lee and Jackson, or Mary and Percy; she even called them John and Yoko once but Vanessa's face grew red quickly because she knew that reference that she never used it again. Ms. Freeman knew, as Vanessa made sure the entire school knew, that she and Keith were dating. Still, Ms. Freeman could not help grouping the best two artists she had ever had.

"I haven't reviewed all your report cards, but I believe it is safe to say in this class that you are all but 45 minutes from being seniors in waiting. In that year you are going to have to make some big choices, so, for this last class I want you to open your pads to draw one more picture. I want you to draw a picture of yourself or what you want to do after next year. Take it home and look at it from time to time, and make sure you fit into the picture. Try to capture how time might have changed you."

Janie had no problem with this. She drew a desk with materials, and scattered dresses on hangers, and a woman at the desk working on a design. Ms. Freeman walked up behind many of the students, studying their pictures. As the bell was about to ring she got to Janie's piece. "Is that you?" Ms. Freeman asked, looking at the picture.

Janie answered sarcastically. "No, I am the cleaning lady about to walk into the picture and clean everything up."

"Well, if that what it takes for you to get into the fashion industry then do it, because one day Janie, I am sure you will be a great designer." By the time Ms. Freeman put down Janie's drawing, it was just about time to bust through the school doors for the last time. Ms. Freeman turned and directed herself to the whole class. "You know, it's not just Janie, I really think all you kids are going to be what you drew today. I don't think I have had a better class of students in some time. You probably won't believe me, but tomorrow as I am heading to clean out the beach cabana, I might just miss you guys. Might, I am not promising, but I might."

A couple of kids tried inviting themselves to the cabana, and Ms. Freeman 'fessed up that she would really not miss them, especially if she were to see them at all during the summer.

As the bell rang the class started to clap and scream. They mixed with cheers from other classes and the General Office which was one door away. Most of the students had learned to get out of teachers' and aids' way on the last day of school as they were usually fleeing the building quicker than the students.

Janie hugged Vanessa and told her she would see her tomorrow for the big game. The Q31 had just pulled up and was waiting for her, but Janie decided to comically break into a mad dash for it one last time anyway.

"Last day of school," she said to the driver as she swiped her card.

The bus driver looked at Janie with a wide smile and said, "Believe me, down at the depot it is all we have been talking about."

The Big Game

"Hey, pop in Deadbolt," Bobby yelled from the backseat as Keith worked his way onto the Long Island Expressway.

"Are you serious?" Keith almost ran into the guard rail as he turned around to see the face of his first NYC convert to the Scariest Band in the World. "What about Psychic Voodoo Doll?"

"Don't mess with me or you'll roast in the flames!" Bobby said, misquoting a line from the song which brought a tear to Keith's eye.

"Winner chooses the music on the way home," Janie added to the bet, while punching Bobby for suggesting Deadbolt.

"One more reason to win," Vanessa said as she lowered the book she was skimming through, reached her arm into the backseat and gave Janie a high five.

"Amo Amas?" Bobby asked, looking at the title of the book that Vanessa was reading. "Is that a book on Latin?" Bobby said kindly, thinking that Vanessa might not have known the topic.

"Ita," Vanessa replied.

"Eh?" Bobby replied, feeling slightly less intelligent than a second ago.

"It is so," Vanessa explained as she continued lecturing. "The Latinites, they had no word for yes, more like phrases confirming truths, or at least that is how it seems to me."

"Isn't what you are doing a form of studying, you know your whole non study mantra." Janie reminded Vanessa of her well noted views on schoolwork.

"It's not school so it doesn't count." Vanessa defended both her learning Latin and belief in doing as little studying as possible in school. "Besides, sooner or later I have to learn something."

"But Latin, you are aware, is a dead language," Janie said, not in a mocking way, but it was said more in a way that was trying to help Vanessa focus her efforts at a better cause. Janie reached and took the book, looking at it, contemplating the meaning to the words on the cover.

"You know Janie, if anybody should understand a language needing to be heard from the grave, I would think it would be you," Vanessa said, smiling, taking the book back from Janie and thumbing through it to the section she was last looking at.

"Post meridium" Bobby said, throwing out his knowledge of Latin in support of Vanessa's point to Janie.

"I was thinking more expo dod," Vanessa replied. "But if you want to talk in simpler terms then fine, post moridium will do."

Keith pulled his car into a spot in field five parking lot of Jones Beach. Bobby had told them to go to field five as it was closest to the volleyball courts. They bounced out of the car to an absolutely beautiful day.

"There is no feeling like the first day at the beach in summertime," Janie said, taking a big breath in. The beach could not be seen because of high sand dunes, but it could be smelt and felt as a strong sun and smell of beach hit their senses once they stepped outside of the car. It wasn't terribly windy, but the essence of salt and sand and a little bit of foam was definitely blowing around in the air. Bobby pointed to a small walkway that ran alongside the West End Bath House. The house was a huge brick building that contained a large pool and gift shop.

"It's so different her," Keith said, as he prepared to take in his first official Beach in New York. "In LA, it's everywhere. I mean, going to the beach is like going over to Bobby's house, it's nothing, but here," he said sadly, "here, it's like a major event to be at the beach."

Vanessa hugged him and said, "Don't worry, we can visit it all the time."

"You don't visit a beach like it's some distant relative," he said. "Can we come back tomorrow?" Keith looked into Vanessa's eyes.

"Sure, as long as you take me and Janie to the mall next week," she said.

"Hey, what is that anyway, a lighthouse?" Keith asked, pointing to the tall structure that was sitting in the middle of the driving circle of the highway road they were just on. The traffic was growing heavier and heavier as more people were making their way to the beach.

"That's the needle," Janie said. "I think it is a lighthouse."

"It's a water tower," Bobby corrected Janie. "It's actually used to pump all the water into the beach facilities."

"Are you serious? It's so skinny.," Keith said in disbelief.

"Yes," Bobby answered. "There is a giant tank in there and it pumps all the water for the park. At least it did in the past, I do not know if it still does. I read on some site they were going to take it down but I am not sure if it's true."

They turned the corner of the bathhouse as Janie continued to look at the needle, saying, "Oh, I hope they don't. I mean, it must be a landmark. It's how I know I am at Jones Beach. It just wouldn't seem the same without it. I mean.. I see that and it reminds me of summer almost more than anything else I can think of."

Keith, who had started the interest in the needle, had completely lost interest, for as they turned the corner he caught a glimpse of the beach. Keith took off and started to run to get closer to the beach. He ran to the top of the steps of the boardwalk and peered out like a captain of a boat looking for another ship or land.

Vanessa ran and caught up with him. "See, there is an East Coast, it's not just a myth."

"It's huge," Keith said. "It's the biggest beach I have ever seen."

"Really?" Vanessa was quite surprised that Keith the California surfer had never seen a beach like Jones. "You should see it when it's packed with people. Sometimes you would think the people are the ocean."

"Come, let's grab a spot by the water," Janie said, as she grabbed Vanessa's hand and they bounded down the stairs. Bobby had also caught up with Keith and he shook the cooler he was now carrying by himself to remind Keith that he could use a little help. Keith grabbed the other end of the cooler as they walked after the girls, who were picking out a spot.

"You think they are ready for it?" Vanessa asked Janie.

"The game? No, we are going to kill them," Janie said confidently.

"I was talking about the secret weapon," Vanessa laughed.

"I don't know about Keith, but I think Bobby is more ready for the game than that," Janie said. "I can't believe you put me up to this." Janie grabbed one end of a blanket as Vanessa grabbed the other.

"Come on, we have been secretly soaking up sun for the last two weeks just for this moment," Vanessa said, offering encouragement.

Janie finished laying down the blankets with Vanessa as the boys arrived at the site. They were able to get a great spot, as the beach was not too crowded due to the wind and threat of rain in the early afternoon, though you could not tell right now as the sun was out and beating strongly down on them. Bobby and Keith dropped the cooler and started to set up the small beach umbrella that Bobby had been lugging in a holder that was slung across his shoulder. "We forgot the ball," he said, as he thrust the bottom part of the umbrella into the sand.

Keith kicked off his sandals and headed down to the beach. He came running back quickly like a scared little girl. "That water is freezing and it's not even clear. It looks like sewer water."

"Hey, they haven't reported hypodermic needles washing up in months," Bobby said, joking around.

"What did you people do to your ocean?" Keith asked, still very upset about his dip in the water. "And what happened to the girls?"

"We're right here." Vanessa's voice came from behind the umbrella. "And we have our secret weapon for the game." As Vanessa made the announcement she jumped out from behind the umbrella in a tight fitting Beach Volleyball outfit. She waited a second looked at Janie, who was still hiding behind the umbrella. She waited one more second, and then grabbed Janie's arm, pulling her into view.

The two girls were dressed in matching, very tight fitting bikini Volleyball outfits. The tops were solid blue with a swooping black line that ran through them. The bottoms again with the line continued on them. Janie started to try to pull the backside down, but felt that the tug just seemed to expose more of her in other spots and just gave up.

"You guys... I mean girls are going to play the game in those?" Keith said, trying to laugh off the intimidation the girls were throwing out.

"What game?" Bobby asked as he let out one little facial tic and continued to stare.

"We are not just going to play you in these; we are going to wipe the floor with you in these," Vanessa said, standing proudly.

Janie, still somewhat crouching and adjusting and picking and stretching the bottoms again, corrected Vanessa. "Wipe the sand or beach she means, can you wipe beach?"

"Well then, it's on," Keith said, still trying not to show any intimidation the girls had built in him. "Bobby, come with me to get the ball, we can talk strategy for the game."

"What game?" Bobby repeated, as Keith pulled him out of his frozen position in front of the girls. Once the boys turned around and headed to the car, Janie started picking at the suit in a

much more deliberate way of attempting to stretch the fabric. Meanwhile Vanessa grabbed the suntan lotion and asked Janie if she noticed Bobby's facial tic.

The talk on the way to the car was more psychological than court inspired and both boys admitted that the girls had already won the first battle. The original plan that Bobby and Keith had drawn up was to spot the girls the first five points by playing poorly, as they did not want them to feel bad. Seeing the girls' confidence level, they lowered it to the first three points that they would dog.

By the time the boys had made it back from the car, Vanessa and Janie were already at a court trying to imaginary spike the ball over the net. Janie had put her T-shirt back on. Keith laughed as he watched Vanessa try to run forward and spike the imaginary ball. He went over and helped Vanessa, showing how jumping on the sand had to be vertical only. Bobby went over to Janie, but he wasn't giving any advice, he took Janie's hand. "Does it hurt?" he asked, pointing to the ball in Vanessa's hand.

"A little," Janie responded. "But don't worry, I will go easy on you."

"To be honest, I am more scared of her," Bobby said, as they both watched Vanessa spike the ball with such force that it kicked up good deal of sand when hitting the ground. Keith retrieved the ball and Bobby joined Keith on their side of the net. At Vanessa's order Janie once again took off her T-shirt. Keith, wanting to show the boys were not completely psychologically overmatched, motioned to Bobby for them to take off their Tee's. Bobby shrugged a second of protest and then joined Keith in removing his shirt.

"I think my eyes are burning," Vanessa joked about the bright light bouncing off Bobby's pale chest and shoulders. Janie pre-served the ball in to the back of her teammate's head lightly to make sure the joking stopped.

"See," Keith said, "look, they are already feeling the pressure. Just keep shaking that body Bobby."

Vanessa picked up the ball and handed it back to Janie, as she stepped outside the rope and prepared to serve. She turned her right shoulder a little toward the net, and bounced the ball. It dropped into the sand with a thud as the boys laughed and asked, What was that?"

Janie ran over to Vanessa. "It doesn't bounce," she said.

"It's sand, Janie."

"But I bounce the ball three times before I serve." As the girls were discussing dealing with the new court surface, the boys were beginning to feel their confidence coming back. They even thought about going back to their original plan of intentionally losing the first five points, but decided to lose three, then decide after that.

Janie and Vanessa worked up a solution and Janie once again stepped outside the ropes to serve. Janie looked at Bobby, who was facing her on the left side of the net.

"ETO," Vanessa said.

"She's speaking Latin," Bobby said to Keith. "I don't like it when [**she] starts speaking Latin."

Janie took a deep breath and pushed the ball downward in a bouncing motion three times while holding onto the ball. She then took to the air and rifled a serve. Bobby barely got a hand on it before it hit his face. His block gave Keith the ability to lob it back over the net, but before Bobby could react again, Vanessa spiked it off his hip.

"That felt good," Vanessa yelled, as she high fived Janie.

"Balls really do like to hit you," Keith laughed out to the bewildered Bobby.

"I told you! It tennis all over again," Bobby said in a defeated tone.

Two points later, as Bobby fetched the ball from another one of Vanessa's spikes, he turned to Keith. "So we are done spotting them points?"

Keith nodded a definitive yes.

"We would not have won any of those points anyway, would we?" Bobby asked, Keith in a low voice.

"Not one." Keith shook his head and leaned closer to Bobby. "I think we might be in trouble."

"We go down like men?" Bobby asked, trying to show he was going to do whatever was needed, as well as leaning on Keith for a plan.

"Yes, exactly. I will pretend to pull something so we have an excuse." Keith proposed the guys' new plan.

Janie and Vanessa were also discussing the game in a huddle, as Vanessa was asking Janie if they should start losing some points intentionally so as to not make the boys feel so bad. Janie ended the huddle saying, "Just make sure we don't lose! I can't listen to that Deadbolt stuff on the way home."

Though the last point did not have the dramatics of the "CUSPIS," it was similar in that Janie passed it to Vanessa, who hammered down a spike which dug into the sand right between Keith and Bobby.

Janie grabbed her shirt from the side of the net and threw it back on as they all headed back to the blankets. Keith, pretending to nurse his pulled quad, walked with a bit of a limp.

"I still say you can't pull your quad playing beach volleyball," Vanessa quipped as she put her arm around the wobbling Keith.

"How else would we have beaten such finely toned male athletes?" Janie added in a very suspicious tone.

"It hurts," Keith defended his antics, as he rubbed the back of his leg.

"What, your leg or your ass from the whipping we gave you?" Janie retorted.

"Or the balls I spiked into Bobby's and your faces," Vanessa added to the list of his possible causes for pain.

"Those hurt," Bobby joined in.

Keith remained silent but his hand snuck behind Vanessa and pulled on part of the elastic part of Vanessa's uniform. It snapped against her back and she yelled out loud. Turning around she tossed the ball at Keith, coming close to hitting him in his swim trunks. The ball bounced off Keith's upper thigh and came to a stop right on one of the groups laid out blankets.

"Oh my poor baby," Janie said in an over the top sincere manner. "Did you hurt yourself too, trying to beat up the big bad girls?" She grabbed the back of Bobby's head and tugged on his left ear as they locked lips and kissed. The kiss lasted several seconds with Bobby wrapping his arms around Janie's bare back. A few seconds later Janie finally pulled away from Bobby. Vanessa, watching the entire romantic moment, started to frown as she lobbed the ball one more time at Keith.

"I want a signature kiss." Vanessa pouted and looked at Keith, who was picking the ball up. "Why don't we have a signature kiss?

Keith dropped the ball and slid next Vanessa. Lowering his voice a little to set the mood he said, "You mean something like this?" Keith wrapped his left arm around Vanessa, holding her firmly in the back. His right hand firmly grasping her shoulder, he tilted his head and brought his lips to Vanessa's. The intensity of Keith's kiss caused Vanessa to shudder slightly before settling down into the soulful kiss.

After several seconds Keith pulled away from Vanessa, who was frozen in her spot.

"Will that do?" he asked.

Vanessa stood there immobile for sometime. Finally she started to move her lips as she said in a very weak voice, "Yes, yes that will do. We will have to test that again later."

Vanessa turned to Janie to see if the time was right, and Janie shook her head yes. "I have something for you," Vanessa said, as she pulled away from Keith and went over and opened her bag. Trying to hide it with her other hand, she turned back to Keith and presented him with a box. "Janie helped me with the box," Vanessa said as she handed it to Keith.

Keith looked at it. He didn't need to open it, the box wasn't identical but the color, a mix of yellow and orange, immediately reminded him of the day at the playground with his mom.

As he started to gingerly open the box, Janie said, "Was that the color? I am pretty sure it was, when I was doing the picture, I wanted so bad to color it that color. Only I didn't have any pencils."

"It's almost the exact color, I don't know what happened to the original," he said, as he pulled the shark tooth necklace out of the case.

"Thank you," Keith said as he gave Vanessa a big hug.

"It's not white, it's not yellow, it went with nothing!" Vanessa said, trying to get Keith a little upset of her reason for returning it, until she finished, "It goes with nothing but you."

Janie waited a little while before calling her over to the blanket and asking her to show her some cool Latin phrases. Janie was still bewildered by the thought that if a sudden Latin quiz broke out at school, that she would need to be cheat off Vanessa's paper.

"Well, there's this one." Vanessa checked her pronunciation and recited, "Hic abundant leones."

"Oh. What's that?" Janie asked.

"It means ']Here lions abound.' They used to put it on maps to scare people."

"I don't think they were trying to scare people," Keith said gingerly. "You know, the Roman empire wasn't so lion-less as it is now."

"Oh well, it was very smart of them then," Vanessa said abruptly.

The Long Way Home

Janie was always tired when she left the beach, probably from the sun beating down on her head and hair all day. As she got in the back of Keith's car for the ride home exhaustion hit. For the first five minutes she barely moved, sitting motionless, she stared out the window. The Long Island Expressway drives right through the center of Long Island and most of the time it allows you to see the surrounding houses and buildings. Janie studied many of them as she finally moved, resting the back of her head on Bobby's shoulder. Bobby noticed that some of the heat that Janie's hair had absorbed at the beach was still trying to escape from her pulled back hair.

"Thank God there will be no Deadbolt on the way home." Vanessa reached over and turned on the radio. As the station came from commercial break it went right into "Lah Lah Lah," which caused Janie to scream, "Put on Deadbolt, put on Deadbolt!"

Keith tried to oblige by attempting to push in the CD, but Vanessa brushed his hand away and turned the radio dial to WPLJ.

Janie settled back down and grabbed a small drawing pad that she had taken to the beach. She started to sketch one house that they had just passed. Lately, Janie was trying to broaden her sketching ability beyond girls and fashion. From her window in her room she would draw the cemetery and even occasionally tried to draw a house. Just like those other times, Janie looked at her drawing with disgust.

I got something to tell you," Bobby said, as he nudged Janie.

Janie slammed down her pencil angrily. Bobby was sure his nudge annoyed Janie until she yelled, "It looks like a box."

Bobby looked at the drawing. "It's nice," he said.

"Nice, if you want to live in a box!" Janie threw her pencil at the drawing. "So, what did you want to tell me?"

"Oh, they are having a fashion drawing contest at my dad's magazine; I have the order form at home," Bobby went on to tell her as Janie picked up her pad and forgot about drawing houses, going back to her fashions. She drew four designs by the time they had exited the Long Island Expressway, and Janie was leaning into the front seat to discuss them with Vanessa.

As they were passing Dominique's, Janie told Keith to drop her off at the back of the cemetery. She wanted to stop by her mom's. Janie was still not sure if her mom could see the drawings, but lately she often passed by when she had drawn something special.

Bobby said he would go with her, but Janie explained that she just wanted to be with her mom alone for a few minutes and that she really needed to take a shower after that.

She kissed Bobby goodbye and jumped out of the car while asking Vanessa one last time what fashion she liked best. Janie bolted into the back entrance of the cemetery. As she got closer to her mom she looked to see if the old lady was around. Janie was relieved to find her nowhere in sight. Since their encounter, the lady would always wave when she saw Janie. She would then pack up whoever she was with and leave, as quickly as possible. Janie felt she did it to respect Janie's time at the site. Even though Janie had divulged little information about how she was related to Alex, she felt the lady knew it was more than just a friendship.

The cemetery, with its shaded trees, was sort of a cool break from the beach where the sun had beaten down on the kids. The day was at that point where it would start to cast shadows in the cemetery and Janie had to move slightly to keep her pad out of one. Janie stayed a little while, touching up her fashions, and seeing if she could get inspiration for one more design from her mom. She did create an additional dress, but liked the one Vanessa had picked out in the car, better than this one as well. The one she had just drawn was too similar to what her mom wore in pictures her father showed her recently. "Sorry mom, but I have to be me," she said, as she packed up her drawing and headed home.

Janie was about half way through the cemetery and looked down the row where Richard Mabbit's marker was. She noticed that a bench was added right by the area. It was a beautiful stone bench, and Janie went over to admire it, feeling that Mrs. Mabbit's new wealth must have influenced its arrival.

The bench was by the tree that Janie originally leaned up against the first time she made contact. Janie admired the plaque with the Mabbits' name listed as the donators.

She brushed some dirt off the bench and sat down; she decided she would try to draw a picture for Mrs. Mabbit. She looked over to Richard's tombstone, and dropped her pencil when she read that the grave was no longer just Richard's.

Janie wanted to get up and go closer to the tombstone, with hopes that it was some sort of illusion, but she knew it wasn't. She just sat there on the bench; she wanted to get up, but all she seemed to be able to do was bring her knees up to her chest. It had been over a month since Mrs. Mabbit had passed, yet, to Janie, it just happened.

It didn't take her long to start crying. Janie had only met her twice, yet, due to everything around their meetings, it seemed like a hundred. She had thought about her so much and often that, to Janie, Mrs. Mabbit was one of her closest friends. Janie cried for a while before picking up her pad. She wanted to do something; something for Arlene. Fighting back tears, she started to draw.

It didn't take more than a second for Janie to realize that she wasn't the one drawing. Janie had been feeling colder and colder, as she was absorbing the shock of what she just learned, but, as she started channeling, the warmth was coming back to her. Janie was concentrating so hard on not influencing the picture that she had no idea of what her current sketch was depicting. As she was finishing, Janie finally started to realize what she was drawing. She waited a second, with her pencil touching the paper, but was pretty sure the caricature was done.

Janie immediately jumped off the bench, and compared it to the drawing. There was no doubt about it; the bench and stone plaque next to it were identical to what Janie had just drawn. Everything was there, like she was looking at the plans Mrs. Mabbit must have drawn up, but, as Janie studied it a little closer, one thing stood out. The star plaque, on the middle column like leg, was different. Janie noticed this and said aloud to herself, "Well, not exactly different, it was just in a different position."

Janie threw down her pad and fell to her knees in front of the leg with the star plaque. Janie didn't have very long nails, as she had a tendency to chew them when she drew. Her lack of nails forced her to have to use her pencil as a wedge to try and move the star into the proper position. Finally, it started to move, and, as she neared the star into the same position of the compartment, she could feel a little latch release. The star and a small box behind it popped out slightly. Janie pulled the box out of its chamber and opened the latch. Inside was a note:

Dear Janie,

Well, it seems that you must have figured out what I knew the first day I met you, that you are a very special artist. I guess you finding this also means I didn't get to see you one last time. I really did hope to see you again.

It always seemed funny to me that things seem to happen so fast or take so long. Well, it took so long to find those tapes, yet, it didn't take long at all for me with my sickness; at least, that is what they are telling me. I fear that I might not see you before it is too late, so I am taking this unusual step to make sure I contact you, and also prove, like I said, that you are special. Janie, the record company gave me much more money than I ever expected, and it helped me and my family so much. I even have something for you, but I am not going to tell you about it until you are 18. For some reason I feel there is someone here who will be able to tell me when that is. I hope you will come back occasionally before then though, for you are such a charming and bright girl. I really do enjoy speaking with you. You also have such beautiful hair! I have thought about you everyday since we met and I can't wait to tell Richard all about you.

Love Always,

Arlene

p.s. You can take this letter to that friend of yours and show him that we weren't crazy.

Janie was trembling as she was reading the letter, but somehow, upon finishing it, she calmed down considerably. When she read the post script, she wanted so badly to tell Arlene that she was dating the doubter. She also wanted to tell her about her mom and her adventures to DC. She wasn't sure if she would be able to, but then she laughed, when she remembered that she had another friend that could get the messages to her, if Janie felt her attempts didn't make it.

Janie had risen from the bench and stood close to the grave. She closed her eyes and said a little prayer. Her children must have planted some flowers, as she again remembered how little she knew about Arlene.

It didn't matter how little she knew, because, like Arlene said, things can happen so fast or slow. It didn't take Janie more than a minute of that first meeting for her to realize that Arlene was a wonderful lady and a best friend.

Janie turned back around to look at the bench. The compartment was still open and Janie bent down to put the compartment back inside the bench. The compartment slid back in with ease. Janie was about to turn the star back into the locking position, but she stopped. Instead, she got up and walked over to her beach bag and riffled through it. Janie grabbed as many drawing pencils as she could dig out of the bag. Also grabbing her pad and sharpener, she rested herself against the tree once again. Janie quickly started drawing, wanting to make sure to start right away to eliminate any chance of her channeling. Once she started, Janie took her time more than she would usually do when drawing people. For a half hour she sat under the tree working on her piece.

Every once in a while she would break from drawing to pull her head a little back from it.

When she was done, she signed it at the bottom; she only did this on very special drawings. Janie studied it one more time before she got up. Getting up wasn't that easy as sitting as she had been in the same stretched out position for a good time, and one of her legs was on its way to falling asleep.

After struggling to get up, and shaking her leg back into action, Janie again headed over to the compartment and slid it out once more. Taking one more look at the drawing to admire it before locking it away, she touched the face of Arlene. She drew her very similar to the first time they met, her hair very short and cropped, and shaded very lightly to allow the grayish white color to be conveyed. She kept her finger on the drawing, following it down the arm of her overcoat, until it reached Arlene's left hand that was interlocked with Richard's.

Janie ran her hand up the young Richard's face, with his cheesy mustache and all. After she got to his face, she pulled back and looked at the two of them. The elder distinguished and lovely Arlene, and the young Lone Star Tornado, guitar slung over his back. They couldn't look happier or more in love. Janie started to tear up as she rolled the drawing up and laid it in the compartment before locking it for good.

The End.....